P9-CFS-600

ESCAPE THIS BOOK!
TITANIC

This book is based on a real event from history . . . but it's not a history book. To put YOU in the action-packed story, true *Titanic* facts and made-up elements are mixed together. Dig deeper into the facts by flipping to the Escapologist Files at the back of the book!

ESCAPE THIS BOOK!
TITANIC

BY BILL DOYLE

ILLUSTRATED BY SARAH SAX & YOU

Random House 🏠 New York

Text copyright © 2019 by William H. Doyle
Cover art and interior illustrations copyright © 2019 by Sarah Sax

All rights reserved. Published in the United States by Random House Children's Books, a division of Penguin Random House LLC, New York.

Random House and the colophon are registered trademarks of Penguin Random House LLC.

Visit us on the Web! rhcbooks.com

Educators and librarians, for a variety of teaching tools, visit us at RHTeachersLibrarians.com

Library of Congress Control Number 2018951842

ISBN 978-0-525-64420-0 (hc)

Printed in the United States of America
10 9 8 7 6 5 4 3 2 1
First Edition

Random House Children's Books supports the First Amendment and celebrates the right to read.

FOR RICCARDO SALMONA

Greetings, my new friend!
There's something you need to know.
Before I tell you . . .

Make hair standing
straight up.

Add super-wide eyes.

Draw a mouth
like an O.

FOLD HERE

When you're done,
fold this
corner
up!

· 1 ·

You are TRAPPED inside this book...
and this book is the TITANIC!

In just a few pages, an iceberg will rip into the side of the *Titanic*, and water will flood inside. Can you escape before it sinks to the bottom of the North Atlantic Ocean?

Who am I? EVERYONE knows me. I am the world's greatest escapologist. I am in search of an assistant for a very special mission. I will tell you more—including my name!—IF you prove yourself worthy by escaping this book. Otherwise, it's just a waste of my very valuable time!

I've sent along my pet gopher, Amicus, to be my eyes and ears during your adventure. He is a master of disguise (not as talented as I am, of course!), and you won't be able to see him until you draw him. I'll let you know when he's around so you can spot him!

I'm Amicus! When you're in a jam, that's where I am!

What does a gopher look like, you ask? A cross between a meerkat and a squirrel!

I predict you'll look just like this when you turn the page and read your fate!

Draw my gopher, Amicus, here.

To survive, you'll need to doodle, demolish, and decide your way out. A sharp pencil or ballpoint pen will help you "pop" through pages when you have to doodle and demolish! Practice your escapology with these three quick challenges.

Demolish!
Quick Challenge #1

Don't hesitate to rip, fold, and scrunch pages when I tell you— every second counts!

How will you reach the crow's nest, which gives the ship's lookouts a view of possible dangers ahead? It's 50 feet above the deck!

Ruin this perfect page by making a small tear along the dotted line and folding the flap up along the gray line.

FOLD HERE

Doodle!
Quick Challenge #2

The *Titanic* will hit an iceberg at 11:40 p.m. on April 14, 1912, and sink two hours and forty minutes later.

Can you spot an iceberg yet?
Or something else?
Draw what you see from the crow's nest.

A ladder inside the ship's mast leads up to a crow's nest. If lookouts see anything, they ring a large bell and call the captain on a wired telephone. Turn the page.

Decide!
Quick Challenge #3

You'll need to make fast decisions to escape this book. The more you know about the *Titanic*, the easier those decisions will be. Lucky for you, I keep detailed files on all of my adventures. In the back of this book, you'll find my Escapologist Files, packed with information you'll need to get out of trouble.

Nearly three football fields long, the <u>Titanic</u> took more than 3,000 people three years to build.

It is the world's most luxurious ship in 1912.

Flip to the page number in my Escapologist Files when you see this folder!

PAGE
175

Let's try out your first decision.
Want to learn more about the <u>Titanic</u> before you begin? Go to page 175.
Or if you think you know enough already, turn the page!

Aces! You've got the basics down.

You're ready to start your great escape. Who will YOU be on this adventure? Before you choose, take a look at who will survive the *Titanic*. The lower your chance of survival, the harder the challenges you will face!

TYPE OF TRAVELER	CHANCE OF SURVIVAL'
First-Class Passengers	61 percent
Second-Class Passengers	42 percent
Third-Class Passengers	25 percent
Crew Members	Less than 25 percent
~~Stowaways~~	Unknown

No one—not even me!—knows these exact numbers for sure.

First class will welcome aboard some of the richest people in the world—bankers, politicians, pro athletes, businessmen—including Isidor Straus, an owner of Macy's department store, and his wife, Ida.

Many third-class passengers are looking for a new life in America—such as a farmer from outside London hoping to plant pecans in Florida, or a family of eight, like the Goodwins, traveling to New York, where Mr. Goodwin plans to work at a power plant.

Choose how you will travel!

Write your name in one of the blanks below.

PASSENGER — Flip to page 56.

WHITE STAR LINE

SECOND-CLASS TICKET for *Dean*

on *the Maiden Voyage of the* RMS Titanic

CREW MEMBER — Go to page 114.

WHITE STAR LINE

APRIL 10, 1912   SHIP: RMS Titanic

CREW MEMBER SIGNATURE: *Esme*

STOWAWAY — Turn the page.

Dean Esme

Best of luck (you'll need it)!

 # STOWAWAY PATH

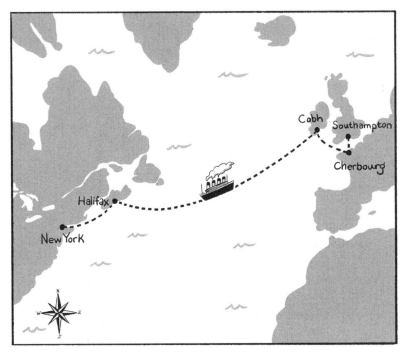

Planned Voyage of the **Titanic**

Remember to flip to the page number here for more information!

You've picked a VERY dangerous path as a stowaway. (No one is 100 percent sure whether people actually stowed away on the ship—and if they did, whether they survived.) But I guess it's worth the risk to you.

PAGE 177

After all, you're a kid trying to escape extreme poverty in northern England, where half your family works in the coal mines. If you can reach your cousin in Boston, you think you can have a better life ... one filled with warmth and FOOD. Oh! Your stomach grumbles just reading that last word, doesn't it? It's all you can think about!

Go to the next page.

Of course, the fare ($350 to $900 in 2019 dollars!) for a third-class ticket on the *Titanic* is way out of your reach. So . . .

At noon on April 10, 1912, just before the *Titanic* leaves port in Southampton, England, for what will be its one and only voyage—you sneak aboard. It isn't too hard, actually. There are 100,000 people on the docks—cheering, waving handkerchiefs, and singing "Rule, Britannia!"

Turn the page.

"All ashore that's going ashore!" Friends and family of passengers were allowed on board to say goodbye. Now all those without tickets must leave the *Titanic* before it sets sail. A crew member might ask for your ticket. You'd better hide!

Dart through the crowd with your pen or pencil
as quickly as you can—without anyone seeing you!

Start here!

End here!

What letter does your path look like?
Write that letter in the Letter Luggage.

Need help?
Go to page 183.

You'll need to carry this with you for a bit!

Go to the next page.

Superb! Now . . . you need somewhere to hide for the planned seven-day journey to New York City. The *Titanic* is 882 feet long (that's one-sixth of a mile); 92 feet wide; and 104 feet high, from the bottom of the ship to the bridge. Plenty of little places to tuck yourself away!

Will you hide in the bridge (the ship's control center) or in one of the lifeboats? Connect the dots to see my hint. Listen to me, I am a Master Escapologist!

Do you take my hint? Turn to page 152.
Or do you ignore my advice? Go to page 13.

You push your way out onto the deck. You're thinking only of your own survival now. You see several boats being lowered—they're not even full!

Shoving people aside, you jump down onto a boat that's halfway to the water. The impact causes the boat to flip, and you and the others plunge into the icy sea. As you sink below the surface, you wonder what would have happened if you had decided to rescue Lightning instead.

END

Go-pher a happier ending. Return to page 151 to pick a different path!

You've chosen to hide in the lifeboat. Wise decision! You have excellent instincts. Maybe you will make your escape after all. We'll see.

When you were sneaking around, you counted only 20 lifeboats. That can't possibly be enough for all the passengers. When something goes wrong, only about half of the 2,200 or so people aboard will be able to fit in lifeboats!

You pull back the cover of the lifeboat just enough to slip inside the front. You lie on the bottom in the darkness—and finally start to relax. The only sound is your stomach grumbling.

Suddenly the cover behind you is peeled back! Are you caught?

No. Two other kids—a boy and a girl—wiggle into the back of the boat. You whisper, "Hello?"

After a moment, the girl replies, *"Tranquillo, sciocco!"*

That's Italian . . . and fairly rude! I think she just called you silly!

To take your mind off being insulted,
give the lifeboat a name and write it here.

Turn the page.

I guess the boy and girl don't speak English. Are they stowaways or just passengers playing hide-and-seek? Either way, there's room for everyone. While some lifeboats on board are smaller or larger, this particular craft is designed to hold 47 people.

You spread out and begin to calm down again when . . .

Something furry scampers over your head! Is that a tail? Is it a rat? A dog?

It's too dark in here to see. Draw what you imagine the creature looks like so I can help you figure out what it is.

14

Go to the next page.

Oh! That is HORRIBLE! You need to get out of this lifeboat NOW. Plus, you need to find something to EAT.

Make sure the coast is clear before leaving the lifeboat. Peer through the opening in the top of the lifeboat. Do you spot anyone or anything that might stop you?

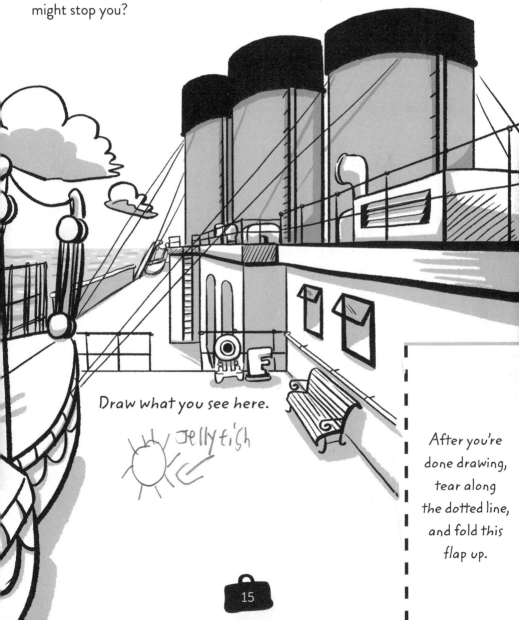

Draw what you see here.

Jellyfish

After you're done drawing, tear along the dotted line, and fold this flap up.

You need to distract whoever's out there before you can escape the lifeboat!

Draw an object you want to fire with the slingshot.
Aim for the bell at the far end of the deck
so it will take attention away from you!

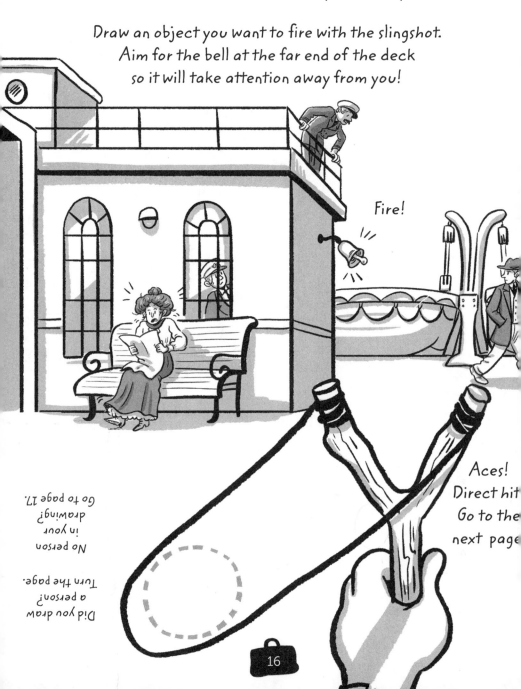

Fire!

Aces!
Direct hit!
Go to the
next page!

No person
in your
drawing?
Go to page 17.

Did you draw
a person?
Turn the page.

16

The coast is clear! You slip out of the lifeboat . . . but where will you go next? Before you can decide, you hear voices and duck behind a corner.

Three men stop nearby. They're arguing about something. But you can't hear exactly what they're saying over the wind.

I know them!

And that's Captain Smith! He looks concerned as he hands Mr. Ismay a note.

That's J. Bruce Ismay, who runs the White Star Line, the company that owns the <u>Titanic</u>!

Who's this? The master-at-arms? If so, he's the man in charge of security and hunting down stowaways . . . like you!

17

Turn the page.

"Do not slow this ship down, Captain," Mr. Ismay commands. Barely glancing at the note, Mr. Ismay tears it up and tucks the pieces in his pocket. A few of the pieces fall to the ground as the men walk off. Curious, you sneak over and pick up the scraps of paper.

To the RMS *Titanic*:

WARNING! DANGEROUS

I C E B E R G S

Put the letter from
your Letter Luggage
on page 10 here!

AHEAD!

This is a marconigram, a telegram or message sent by radio-telegraphy. This is how many ships communicate with each other in 1912. They don't send actual letters or words using the devices. They use Morse code, a series of dots ● ● ● and dashes ▬ ▬ ▬ that represent letters. Interesting, yes?

Pieces of the message are missing. Can you fill in the blanks?

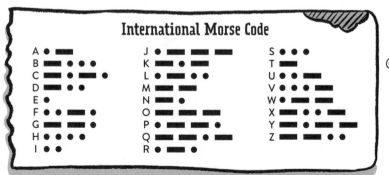

International Morse Code

A ● ▬	J ● ▬ ▬ ▬	S ● ● ●
B ▬ ● ● ●	K ▬ ● ▬	T ▬
C ▬ ● ▬ ●	L ● ▬ ● ●	U ● ● ▬
D ▬ ● ●	M ▬ ▬	V ● ● ● ▬
E ●	N ▬ ●	W ● ▬ ▬
F ● ● ▬ ●	O ▬ ▬ ▬	X ▬ ● ● ▬
G ▬ ▬ ●	P ● ▬ ▬ ●	Y ▬ ● ▬ ▬
H ● ● ● ●	Q ▬ ▬ ● ▬	Z ▬ ▬ ● ●
I ● ●	R ● ▬ ●	

Need help?
Go to page 183

18

Go to the next page.

You read the message and gasp. How could an iceberg be a danger to the *Titanic*? Surely nothing could sink this mightiest of all ships . . . could it?

Hmm. Do you really need me to answer that?

Wait a second. You saw TWO men walk away. Where is the third? The master-at-arms is still somewhere in the area! He could catch you at any second!

You slip back into the shadows and wait for the sun to go down. You're cold, and you imagine what it would be like to put up a tent and just sleep here. Don't forget the campfire to cook up some FOOD!

Draw your tent below. Then turn the page.

Aces! Real shame that tent isn't real. BUT while you were drawing it, the master-at-arms wandered off.

So no more dillydallying! Time to hunt for an actual bed. There should be loads of empty cabins. After all, the *Titanic* can carry 3,500 people, but there are only about 2,200 passengers and crew on this maiden voyage.

Sticking to the shadows, you creep inside, go down a flight of stairs, and find yourself alone in the most beautiful hallway you've ever seen. You're on B deck—mostly for first-class passengers! The deep carpet is soft under your feet. You can't believe that people walk on this with their dirty shoes.

Bright lamps with reflective mirrors illuminate the hallway. Someone could spot you at any second! You need to hide, maybe in one of the cabins that line both sides of the hallway.

Go to the next page.

You gently tap on the nearest door—ready to run if you hear footsteps from inside. There's no response. Is this one empty? It could be a great hiding spot. You crouch to peer through the keyhole.

Poke your pen or pencil through the keyhole. What do you see?
Looks like stars to me.
Do you decide to go in?

If yes, turn to page 23.
If no, turn to page 24.

The shouting has alerted the master-at-arms! He must've been following you, because he's in the cabin in a flash!

Turn to page 130.

22

You open the unlocked door just a crack, squeeze inside, and find a man standing in his moon-and-stars pajamas. The man is furious, and he starts shouting!

Oh! I can't look. Can you draw an expression on his face?

After you're done drawing, go to page 22.

You don't go into the cabin. Something doesn't feel quite right. Besides, you think someone might be following you. Better keep moving!

Is that the shadow of the master-at-arms?
Draw him in the hall! (Do you remember what he looks like?
For a reminder, flip back to page 17.)

In which direction should you run
to get away from the master-at-arms?

Run right—go to page 26.
Run left—go to page 130.

24

The wealthy passenger is furious with your decision. After she complains to your boss, you are demoted to cleaning kitchen drains.

What's the most disgusting thing you can imagine?
Draw it here. Tear along the dotted lines
and fold over the flap after you're finished.

Don't give up! Head back to your last decision and **go-pher** it!

Did you come with a dog named Flealight? Go back to page 121.

Said "No thanks!" to the bellhop job? Return to page 123.

You run right, away from the master-at-arms. You race back to the stairwell and down to the next deck. You dash through corridors and run up and down different staircases as you sneak around nearly all of the *Titanic*'s ten decks meant for passenger use.

And soon find yourself lost. The ship is beyond confusing! There are miles of corridors on the *Titanic*, and each deck is laid out differently than the one below.

This is what you're holding four days later, when the *Titanic* strikes an ← iceberg and sinks!

At one point, you're creeping down the corridor that's known as Scotland Road. It's named after the longest street in Liverpool, England, which is the ship's home port. The hallway runs nearly the full length of the *Titanic*. That makes it longer than the height of a tower on San Francisco's Golden Gate Bridge (which will be built in about 25 years).

END

Draw in the rest of the Golden Gate Bridge here.

Go to the next page.

Still feeling that you're being chased, you slip past crew members who are standing guard outside the gate that leads to the accommodations of the third-class passengers. (The guards are there to stop those passengers from going to the decks above.)

To you, it's still pretty fancy down here, but everything and everyone seems more casual. Some third-class passengers have left their doors open. Most of the simple rooms have at least two bunk beds—some have three. Unfortunately, there's always at least one person in each of the rooms, so there's nowhere to hide!

You know you can't keep running much longer. You're exhausted . . . and hungry!

Imagine you could just slip inside one of these cabins and relax. Draw what you would do. When you're finished, turn the page!

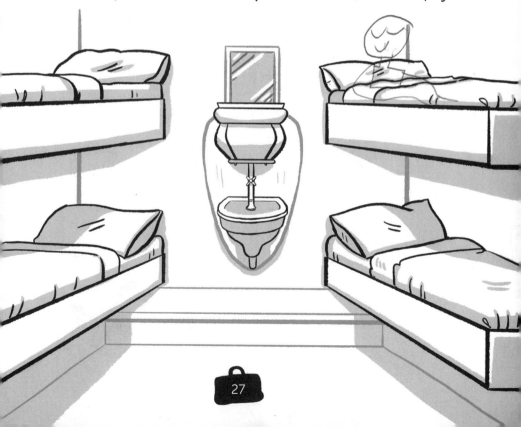

You pop your head into what turns out to be the public lavatory. You see that the toilets automatically flush down here, but they don't do that in first class. Why is that?

PAGE 179

In the hallway, a delicious smell wafts your way. Following your nose, you head toward the dining saloon, or cafeteria, where you hope to blend in.

DINNER MENU

Rice soup
Fresh bread
Biscuits
Roast beef with gravy
Sweet corn
Boiled potatoes

For dessert:
Plum pudding with sweet sauce
Fruit

I know, I know! You're starving. But there's no time to put things __in__ your face. Put them __on__ it as a disguise.

Go to the next page.

28

"Nice try," a deep voice says next to you.

It's the master-at-arms—and he sees through your food costume right away.

Before he can grab you, you run again! Back up and up and up you go. You reach C deck, and suddenly you're in the crew area, where officers and stewards alike can relax. Crew members look up from their newspapers and tea in surprise when you burst into the room.

Definitely not a good plan. You can't go back the way you came. The only other way out is a door in the far wall that leads to a hollow upright tube.

Quick! Draw the rungs of a ladder up the tube. . . .
Now draw yourself climbing the ladder! Then turn to page 132.

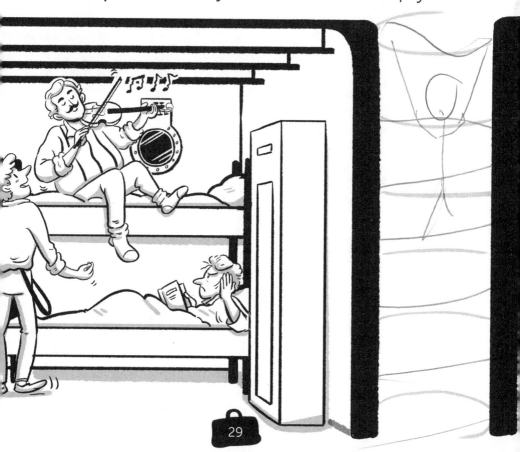

29

You head to F deck, of course! On the way to the kennel, you stop at the poop deck (hee-hee) to give Lightning a chance to exercise . . . and, well, you know the name of the deck.

PAGE 175

When you arrive at the kennel, the crew member in charge, Louis, takes Lightning by the collar. There are about ten dogs down here already, locked in large cages that line one wall. Some passengers must be keeping their dogs in their cabins—lucky mutts!

Louis gently puts Lightning in his cage and locks it. You watch him open and shut the cabinet on the wall as he puts away the key. But you barely notice. You're too worried about Lightning. He begins to whimper immediately. You don't want the poor pup to be lonely.

Draw a dog toy for Lightning—something to keep him company.

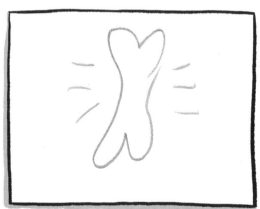

You push the dog toy between the bars of his cage. Lightning takes it gently in his mouth, wags his tail, and curls up in the way back of the cage. Aces! He won't be so lonely down here anymore!

Turn to page 134.

With the master-at-arms still holding your shoulder, you glance over the railing at the endless gray waves. That cold water could kill you in just a few minutes.

"Do you throw stowaways overboard?" you ask.

The man laughs. "I'm not the master-at-arms, if that's what you're thinking. I'm Chief Engineer Joseph Bell. What's your name?"

At first you lie and tell him a fake name.

"I'm _____Otter_____ _____Cherios_____," you say.

Quick! ↗
Think of the name of
a pet you know!

↖ And what's your
favorite cereal?

Mr. Bell laughs again. Finally, you tell him your real name and that you're from the coal country of Northumberland, in England.

Joseph Bell squints at you. "Northumberland, you say?" he asks doubt-fully. "I'm from there, too. Prove it. Show me your house."

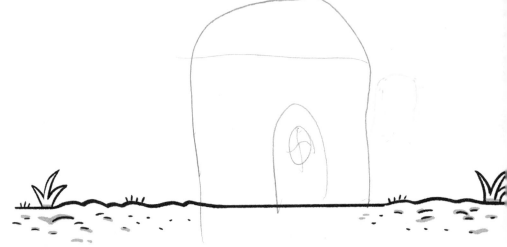

Draw your house here.
Go to the next page.

"Hmm," the chief engineer says. "I don't recognize the house, but I do recognize something about your face. I think I know your family. They've been mining for generations. Coal is in your blood, am I right?"

You nod.

"Good," he says. "I'll give you two choices. I can turn you over to the actual master-at-arms, who will lock you in the brig. That's what we call the jail on a ship. When we arrive in America, he'll send you back to England on the first boat. Or . . . you can earn your passage by working for me as a coal trimmer in the engine room for the rest of the voyage. I could use the help."

Seems like an easy choice, right?

Wait! You're going to want to go to the back of the book before you make this decision!

PAGE
180

If you turn down the chief's job offer, turn to page 130.

Want to work in the engine room? Turn the page.

33

Even though trimmers receive the worst pay and have the worst work conditions of the engineering crew, you choose that option.

After you agree to be a trimmer, Mr. Bell gets you a plate of stew and a biscuit—YUM! FINALLY! Then you follow him through a maze of tucked-away stairwells and locked doors to the engine room, deep in the bowels of the ship, two stories below the waterline.

"We're the ship's little secret," Mr. Bell says. "We have our own hidden passageways so the paying customers don't have to lay eyes on us. We even sleep and eat in separate sections from them."

You're a member of the "black gang" now. That's what the 350 or so men who are in charge of running the engines call themselves because of the dark soot and thick coal dust in the air down here.

Draw yourself in the engine room!

34

Go to the next page

The heat, the noise . . . especially the overwhelming din of the giant engines at work—it's almost too much. You wonder if some of the men stuff cloth in their ears to block the sound.

Draw a machine or an animal that makes a lot of noise.
Then tear along the dotted lines and fold over the flap.

Turn the page.

Mr. Bell takes you to a LOUD, HOT boiler room and introduces you to another trimmer, who's about 20 years old. "This is Matteo," Mr. Bell tells you. "He'll get you set up."

Matteo gives you a friendly smile, says *"Ciao"*—that's *hello* in Italian—and hands you a shovel.

For the next day, you work inside a dimly lit, dust-filled, searing-hot coal bunker, shoveling coal down chutes to the boilers just below. Firemen there load it into the 29 boilers and 162 furnaces that burn about 650 tons of coal a day, generating 16,000 horsepower that keep the ship moving at its top speed of 23 knots (about 26 miles per hour).

Did you get all that?

I'm not done with your list of duties yet!

Multiply that sound by, I don't know, a billion! That's how noisy it is in the engine room.

You also need to haul away the ash from the boilers. First cool it with water from a hose and then cart it over to the ash ejectors that use high-pressure jets of water to fire it into the ocean.

One of the most important jobs of a trimmer: You must keep the coal level in the bunkers or the ship will list to the side.

Go to the next page.

Tear along the dotted lines and fold up the flap below to show the level of the water.

"Oh, that's not right," Mr. Bell says. "I think I picked the wrong kid for this job." Turn to page 171.

Mr. Bell is impressed with your work! For the past two days, you've really proven yourself to be a hard, smart worker.

All right, all rig
I am, too . . . at l
a little bit.

And on the evening of April 14, the chief has a more complicated challenge for you—a mystery to solve. "A fire was discovered in the coal bunker before we left port," he tells you. "We keep finding branches of it but don't know exactly where it's coming from."

PAGE
180

"A fire? Running loose on a ship?" you say. "That can't be good."

"It's fairly contained in the bunker . . . for now," Mr. Bell responds. "Fires in coal bunkers can be like branches on a tree. You have to follow the line of the fire along the branch back to the trunk to find the source. Make sense?"

After you nod, he continues. "Other trimmers have been trying to trace the source of the fire and extinguish it—without luck. Can you help them?"

Go to the next page.

Which side should you and the other trimmers shovel FROM in order to straighten out the Titanic?

If you shovel FROM the right, turn the page.

If you take the coal FROM the left, turn down the corner above.

Follow the line through the tangle of flame, and turn back the flap when you've located the source of the fire.

Start here

You followed the wrong path.
And Mr. Bell is not pleased!
Go to page 171.

"Bully for you!" Mr. Bell shouts, and slaps you on the back like a proud uncle. He looks at his watch. "It's nearly eleven-forty now," he says—

Did he just say 11:40? I'm sorry to interrupt, but you might want to hold on to something.

—to the senior officer. "I want this fire out in the next few hours."

Mr. Bell is still explaining his plan to extinguish the fire thirty seconds later, when a red light on the wall illuminates the word *STOP*.

That light can only be turned on by the bridge. All the engineers burst into action to stop the engines.

Why is Captain Smith ordering the engines to be shut down?

If you want to barrel ahead with your escape all willy-nilly, go to page 42.

If you want to see the action that led to the captain's order to stop, turn to page 140.

You found the source! It's in the No. 6 boiler room. Turn the page.

You pop the postcard into the envelope for Mrs. Mortimer's mother-in-law and seal it. You put a stamp on it that looks like this:

Draw your stamp here!

Just as you're placing the envelope on a pile of mail near the door, the postal clerks all start moving at once. "We're closing up for the next thirty minutes," the American says. He explains that when a Royal Mail Ship sets sail, postal clerks begin distributing mail to the passengers.

The clerks hustle you out of the sea post office as they push carts filled with mail past you.

You're left standing in the hallway holding the photograph of the nanny on the electric camel. That's when you realize you've made a HORRIBLE mistake. You put your postcard in the envelope to Mrs. Mortimer's mother-in-law.

"Wait!" you shout to the clerks. "I need to get that envelope back!" But it's too late. They've disappeared around the corner. What do you do?

You figure Mrs. Mortimer will understand that you made a mistake.
Turn to page 170.

You decide to find a way to break into
the sea post office to fix your mistake. Go to page 141.

"Something doesn't feel right," you're about to say, when—

—the iceberg tears through the hull of this section of the ship! Your true escape has begun.

Draw the iceberg.
Remember, a big part of the iceberg is underwater!

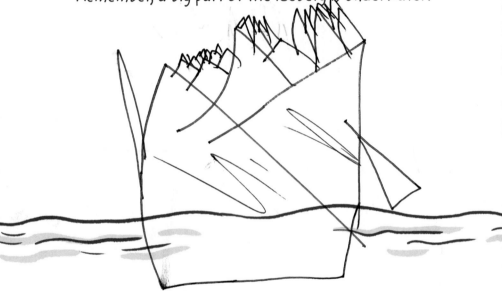

Go to the next page!

Men are pulled under as seawater floods into the ship, but you, Mr. Bell, and the other officer escape through the connecting tunnel to the No. 5 boiler room. Quick! Close the bulkhead doors so water doesn't rush into this room, too!

Draw a thick steel bulkhead door here
to block the rising water from coming into the room.

What can you add to make it stronger?
Draw a wheel on the door you create, so that you can lock it shut.

Turn the page.

You manage to close the door, preventing the water from following you . . . for now.

Up in the bridge, the captain has ordered more watertight doors to be sealed. These doors are located around the ship and can be closed in an attempt to prevent flooding.

Watertight doors each weigh about a ton, and it takes a few seconds for them to be lowered by machinery.

You have ten seconds to pull your pen or pencil through these four holes at the same time or you will be stuck inside this room. Time yourself and give it a try!

Did you make it through in time? Turn to page 46.
Didn't quite make it? Go to page 101.

You burst back onto the port side of the boat deck. Because the early boats were lowered only half-full, these final lifeboats are overfilled and might swamp. Soon people are pushing. Someone fires a gun in the air, trying to get people to stand back and calm down. You still can't find your dad, but shouting catches your attention.

A young boy about your age is trying to get onto a boat with his mother. But an officer in charge won't let him aboard. The officer says that the boy is 13, and that's old enough to leave school and get a job—that makes him a man.

PAGE 176

You and the boy's father argue with the officer. And as the *Titanic*'s bow sinks deeper into the ocean, the officer seems to realize there isn't any more time. "Fine," he says. "But no more exceptions for boys or men."

You don't bother trying to get on the boat—you're holding on to the hope of locating your dad. And guess what? You do! As the last of the lifeboats is lowered into the sea, you run to the other side of the deck and find your dad.

You two hug as the *Titanic* continues to sink.

END

I don't **go-pher** sad endings! Return to page 100 and try again!

Phew! You made it through in time! But you're not done yet.

"Right now, the *Titanic* is four hundred miles from land, with over two thousand people on board in the freezing-cold waters of the Atlantic," Mr. Bell is saying into the phone at midnight. He's talking to the bridge, telling Captain Smith that the ship cannot stay afloat with this kind of damage—it will sink in a couple of hours.

The captain gives the order for the lifeboats to be uncovered and for all passengers and crew to make their way to the boat deck.

46

Most of the engineering crew decide to remain below deck. Some keep the generators running to power the ship's lights. Other crew members are fighting to keep the ship afloat by operating the pumps.

Each boiler room has a pump to suck out water, but the valves in this boiler room are blocked by lumps of coal. Because these blocked valves are underwater, you're going to have to clear away the lumps of coal without looking.

Examine this picture carefully. Now close your eyes and draw three Xs where you think the coal might be. I've done a fourth one for you!

I'm trusting you to be honest!

Turn the page.

47

Aces! Your work has helped to slow down the *Titanic*'s sinking.

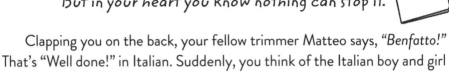

PAGE 181

But in your heart you know nothing can stop it.

Clapping you on the back, your fellow trimmer Matteo says, *"Benfatto!"* That's "Well done!" in Italian. Suddenly, you think of the Italian boy and girl who climbed into the lifeboat with you four days ago.

Were they stowaways like you? What if they don't speak any English? You need to warn them to get off the ship. You explain the situation to Mr. Bell.

"Go, go!" he tells you. "You've done all you can do here. Good luck!"

You think he's one of the bravest men you've ever met.

Draw the statue of him you'd like to put up in a park someday.

Go to page 167.

You and the lifeboat are flung 50 yards. The smokestack actually did you a favor. You're now clear of the suction of the sinking ship!

PAGE 177

You gasp as it disappears under the surface of the water.

Balancing on the upside-down lifeboat, you call to others who might be swimming out in the darkness. Three people shout back, and you help them onto the boat with you.

One of the passengers has a blanket. She suggests you wave it as a banner to get the attention of rescuers.

You don't have an oar to attach to the blanket. But you do have your Tip-O-Meter! You can hoist the blanket with that. Will it be high enough to get noticed?

Jab a hole here with your pencil or pen, roll up your Tip-O-Meter so it's like a long tube, and pull it through the hole and wave.

Draw yourself on the lifeboat!

Do you have fewer than five coins? Turn the page.
At least five coins on your Tip-O-Meter? Go to page 85.

You can't raise the blanket high enough in the air!

The people in nearby lifeboats fail to see you. The current carries you and your fellow passengers away from the site of the sinking.

When rescuers arrive just a short time later, you're nowhere to be found!

END

I'll give you a tip for being so close to your escape!
Add two coins from me to your Tip-O-Meter
and go back to page 49.

Don't say I never gave you anything!

You look around the deck. You see a life jacket, a folding chair, and some rope.

In the first box, draw how you would use these
three items as a flotation device to make your escape!

(1)

(2)

When you're done,
tear along the dotted lines
and fold over this flap.

Holding the life jacket tied to the chair, you jump into the water.

You plunge below the surface for a terrifying few seconds. The temperature takes your breath away, and you see how this cold water could kill someone in just minutes.

You've lost hold of the raft you made. There it is! You can barely see it in the darkness. You swim to it and flip it over so the life jacket is under the folded chair. Then you pull yourself up out of the water. Thanks to the way you tied the life jacket under the chair, you're floating above the killer cold water.

You can't stay balanced up here for long—you need help . . . right away. You start shouting, hoping that people in a nearby lifeboat will hear you.

And guess what?
Turn to page 54.

Did you tie the life jacket
to the chair?

If yes, turn to page 52.

If no, try drawing your flotation
device again, in the second box,
before you turn the page!

Draw yourself here!
↙

You jump! As you're falling through the air, you know that you're going to hit the lifeboat too hard. And you're right.

When you land on the side of the boat with an *oomph*, the impact tips it, and you tumble out of the boat.

As you hit the surface of the icy water below, you think, *If I could do it all again, maybe next time I'd invent my own escape!*

END

Why not give that a try? **Go-pher** a different path on page 168!

A lifeboat makes its way over to you, and its passengers pull you on board.

Draw yourself on the lifeboat, happy to be safe!
Turn to page 172.

54

PASSENGER PATH

So you picked *second-class passenger*—and the best odds of survival! Only first class would give you a better chance, but that's not one of my options.

Mwah-hah-hah!

Well, I'm not going to make your escape easy for you. (No one ever did ME any favors when I was escaping from a milk carton in that submerged cave in Portugal!)

For this choice, you're someone who likes adventure and LOVES music—all sorts of 1912 music—ragtime, classical, and catchy popular songs! As you wait for the *Titanic* to set sail, you hear and see rhythm everywhere you look. You can even feel the ship's humming engine through your feet, like it's the world's biggest musical instrument.

Find these hidden musical notes #1 and #2 in this picture.

Count how many of each type of note you find. Write the totals in the blanks to learn what page to turn to next!

Flip to page _____ _____.

music note #1   music note #2

57

Need help?
Go to page 183.

Who knows?
Someday ALL those things in the catalog could be yours!

Your family is hoping for a better life in America, where your dad will teach music and play in a friend's restaurant. Your mom and little brother already sailed on a regular old ship to New York City—the *Titanic*'s planned destination. They went over two weeks ago. But your dad knows how much you love ships, so he invited you to travel with him on the greatest ship ever built.

When your dad told you about the *Titanic*, you did a little happy dance!

Draw your favorite dance move here.
Break it down into three steps.

Step One   Step Two   Step Three (the big finish!)

Go to the next page.

Right now, the *Titanic*'s main deck is PACKED with passengers and crew members. Everyone is facing the dock, where a 100,000-person crowd is cheering and waving.

As the tugboats get in position to push and pull the ship away from the dock, the crowd starts singing "Rule, Britannia!"—a British patriotic song. Your dad and other musicians in his orchestra decide to play along. But where's your dad's violin?

"I need help fast!" your dad says. You don't want him to get fired already—you'd get booted off the boat right now!

Draw a violin (or any instrument!) in his hands.

59

Turn the page.

Well done! Your dad has never sounded better—

Wait! Who's that?

You spot a kid darting through the crowd. That kid looks to be up to something. And that something could be adventure! Do you follow?

Yes, absolutely! Turn to page
Um, no thanks. Go to page 16

I'm sad to say that your plan will only make your situation worse.

You scramble up the deck as it rises more and more into the air. Soon it's nearly vertical—it's like you're trying to climb a wall. You grab on to a railing for support and hang on!

Chairs, luggage, life jackets—everything slides past you and gets sucked underwater as you desperately hang on.

You know you won't be able to keep your grip on the railing much longer. In just a few seconds, you'll let go and slide down toward the water. . . .

END

I can't watch! **Go-pher** that one more time. Turn back to page 160!

Aces! You've proved you can follow the music—
this might be what allows you to escape in the end.

There's your dad!

These four other men are in the five-piece orchestra
with your dad. Many musicians will be on board!

62

Go to the next page.

Your dad's been hired to play music for passengers by the White Star Line. That's the company that built and owns the RMS *Titanic*. Your dad will get paid, BUT he's not counted as a crew member.

What's the best part? You get to travel with him as a second-class passenger! Your family could never swing the thousands of dollars for just one first-class ticket, but your dad scraped together the $60 for your fare. (That's about $1,400 in 2019 dollars!) And you couldn't be more thankful. After all, second class on the *Titanic* is like first class on most other ocean liners!

What would you pick from this catalog page with the thousands of dollars you'd save between a first-class and second-class ticket on the *Titanic*?

Draw the missing items here!

MOST ASTOUNDING GIFTS of 1912

FORD TOWN CAR
$800

WRIGHT BROTHERS' 1908 MODEL A FLYER
$25,000

FOUR-PASSENGER HOT-AIR BALLOON
$2,000

TOY ELECTRIC TRAIN SET
$6.98

63

Turn to page 58.

PAGE
175

The kid sneaks toward the port side of the ship. You're following just a few steps behind . . . but when you turn the corner, the deck over here is empty!

How is that possible? The kid couldn't have just disappeared! You look around for a good ten minutes, when you notice that a man has wandered onto the deck.

That's J. Bruce Ismay! He's head of the White Star Line and pretty much owns the *Titanic.* His eyes flick over the LIFEBOATS—you can almost see him counting them—before he heads back inside. Mr. Ismay is the man responsible for limiting the number of LIFEBOATS on board the *Titanic.* He thought having more LIFEBOATS would just clutter things up.

Are you getting the HINT yet?
Where do you look for the missing kid?
At the top or the bottom of this page?
Tear along the dotted line and
fold over the flap in that spot!

65

You're not listening to me!
Go to page 161!

Hmm. That's strange.
I thought that other kid was in here!

Inside the lifeboat, you find eleven-year-old twins—a boy and a girl—who don't speak English. Why are they hiding?

"*Ciao!*" the boy chirps, but the girl seems exasperated and hisses at you, "*Cos'hai che non va? Chiudere il coperchio!*"

Isn't that Italian? Good thing you speak a little. You played Antonio the aardvark in an Italian opera. You try singing some of it to them.

"*È la tua testa di formaggio?*" the girl says with a playful smile.

I think she asked if you're full of cheese. . . .

You need something to lure the twins out of the lifeboat so you can talk to them. Maybe the poster from the Italian opera *Aardvarks on the Ferris Wheel* would do the trick?

Draw it here.
Make sure it's got an aardvark
and a Ferris wheel!
When you're done,
go to th age.

Look at that!
Two for the price of one!
Turn the page.

So am I.

The twins seem confused. But they climb out of the lifeboat anyway.

"*Polizia?*" the girl asks you.

"No, I'm a passenger," you say.

Ah! They're wondering if you're with the police.

"Are you with the police?"

They give you a long look. The girl glances at her brother and rolls her eyes. "*Questa persona non è intelligente.*"

The language barrier is going to be tough.

Without using any real words, draw this question for them:
"*Are you stowaways?*"

Finished drawing? Turn the page.

"No!" The twins laugh and shake their heads.

"Dante," the boy says, and points at himself, then at his twin. "Nicola."

After a moment, Nicola gives you a friendly nod. She holds up three fingers and then gestures at herself and her brother.

Oh! They're third-class passengers. Those passengers are mostly immigrants like you, moving to America for a better life. Third-class cabins are on the lowest decks and separated from second class by gates. The White Star Line says that's to keep immigrants from coming into the country undocumented.

1. Draw the path from the lifeboat to your cabin, making sure to pass through all the stars.

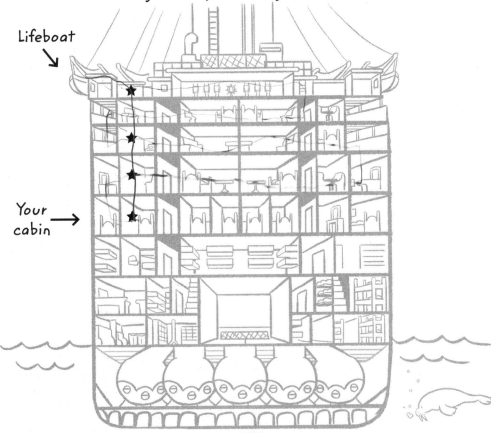

Lifeboat

Your cabin →

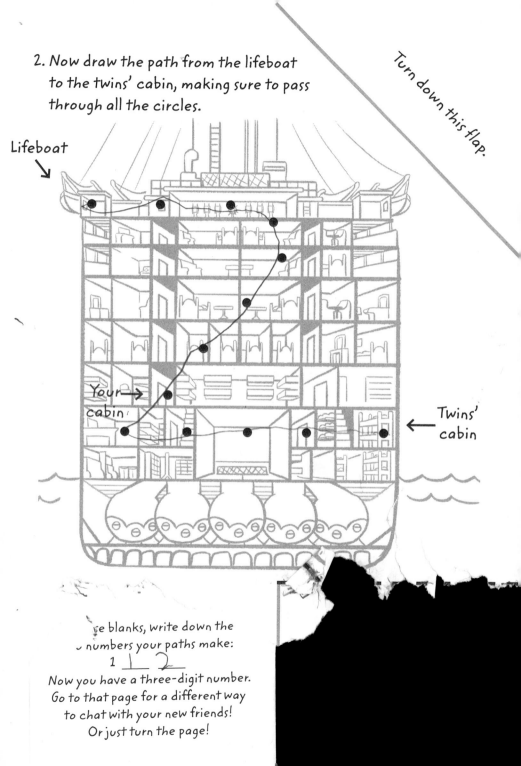

2. Now draw the path from the lifeboat to the twins' cabin, making sure to pass through all the circles.

Lifeboat

Your → cabin

Twins' cabin

Turn down this flap.

se blanks, write down the
numbers your paths make:
1 ___ 2 ___
Now you have a three-digit number.
Go to that page for a different way
to chat with your new friends!
Or just turn the page!

Passengers toward the top of the Titanic (those in higher classes) are closer to the lifeboats and are more likely to survive in the event of an emergency.

After you introduce yourself to the twins, Nicola beams and says your name with a wonderful Italian accent.

You and the twins draw pictures for each other. Soon you figure out that they snuck up from third class (with their mom's okay) and were planning to hide in the lifeboat until dark. They want to explore the ship's galleys, or kitchens.

"Why?" you ask, surprised. "Are you hungry?"

They shake their heads. No, that's not it. For some reason, they blush and draw that they'll tell you later. In the meantime, they would love to see the kitchen up here in second class!

You offer to help them find it! There's no reason to wait for nightfall. You have a second-class ticket, and if anyone asks, you can just explain that the twins are with you. After some wrong turns in the maze of corridors, you and the twins find the galley shared by the first- and second-class dining saloons.

On the floor outside the kitchen, you find a list of food supplies. Jackpot! The twins would think it is fascinating. But the list is in English.

Over 60 chefs and their assistants work in the Titanic's five galleys, including soup chefs, pastry chefs, and a kosher chef.

70

Go to the next page.

Everything the chefs need to make thousands of meals during the voyage had to be on board when the ship left port. Draw pictures of the following things so Nicola and Dante can be wowed by the huge numbers, too.

75,000 pounds of fresh meat	7,000 heads of lettuce
36,000 oranges	1,500 gallons of fresh milk
1,000 loaves of bread	40 tons of potatoes

71

When you're finished, turn the page!

For the next two days, as the *Titanic* sails through the North Atlantic, you explore with the twins. There's so much to see on the ship!

Sure, second class doesn't offer quite as many fun things to do as first class. But there are deck games like ringtoss, the second-class library, board games like backgammon—and (your favorite) so much music EVERYWHERE!

Right now you're enjoying a bagpiper's version of "The Man on the Flying Trapeze" and playing shuffleboard with the twins on the poop deck.

PAGE 175

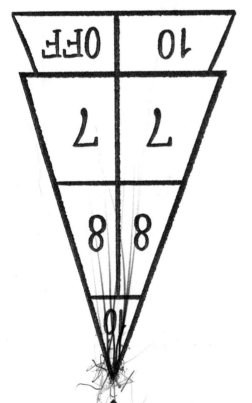

Put the tip of your pen here!

PEN SHUFFLEBOARD!

1. Put the tip of your pen or pencil by the arrow below the shuffleboard court.

2. Place just one finger at the top of the pen.

3. Push! Did you land on a number?

4. Repeat four more times.

What's your total score? Try to beat it!

Go to the next page.

While you play shuffleboard, a young crew member hurries by. The bellhop is holding a small dog and trying to feed it a treat. "Why won't you eat this, Lightning?" the bellhop says.

"*Vuole che io non abbiu peli sulla lingua?*" Dante calls after the bellhop. The twins turn to each other and talk about a recipe for delicious dog treats.

After just two days with the twins, you've picked up a few words of Italian, so you can understand a little of what they're saying.

"What did you mean by what you said to the bellhop?" you ask Dante. "Something about 'without hair on the tongue'?" But even as you ask it, the meaning becomes clear. "You were asking if the bellhop wants your honest opinion! That's something you would say to a friend, right? Like we are."

"Yes . . . we are friends," Nicola says in English. The twins finally seem ready to tell you what they were too embarrassed to say before. They create a rebus for you:

Write what they're saying here.

We want to be chefs in America

Then turn to page 158.

Need help?
Go to page 183.

You scan the boats. There! The Mortimers are on one of the lifeboats, waiting to be lowered into the water. The crew has allowed Mr. Mortimer, the valet, and the butler on the lifeboat, even though they're men. Lucky!

Lightning's tail thumps against your chest when he sees them. You hand him down to Mrs. Mortimer's waiting arms.

"Thank you," she says. She gives you that same wink she gave you when you first met. "I knew I picked the right one," she says with a smile. "Quick, get on board . . . there's plenty of room. The lifeboat is half-full."

It's true. Only 27 of the 65 seats are filled. Before you can move, you're pulled back by your boss, and the other crew members start to lower the boat.

Mrs. Mortimer shouts, "No!"

But it's too late; you're being pushed back and the boat is going down.

Something shiny turns in the air. You reach out and grab it. It's a coin from Mrs. Mortimer. You know just what she is saying: *Stay alive for yourself . . . and for your sister.*

Add the coin to your Tip-O-Meter!

Go to the next page.

Why was the Mortimers' lifeboat lowered when it was only half-full?

You're determined to make sure the same thing doesn't happen again.

You spend the next twenty minutes helping others onto the lifeboats. You watch as people say goodbye to each other. It's horrible and so sad.

To stay strong, draw what makes you feel brave here.

Turn to page 160.

Monster Adventure

Sea monster!
Go back to **START.**

WHAT YOU DO:

1. You can play alone, taking turns for YOU and YOU #2. Or invite a friend or two to play. The person with the shortest hair goes first.

2. Grab buttons, beads, or whatever's on hand to use as gondola playing pieces—one for each player. Place them on START.

3. When it's your turn, flip two coins. If you flip . . .
—HEADS & TAILS, move ahead one space.
—TWO HEADS, move ahead two spaces.
—TWO TAILS, move ahead three spaces.
Follow the directions on the space.

4. The next player takes a turn. Play continues until a player reaches FINISH. That player wins!

Move ahead **1** space.

Canal creature pops up! Lose your next turn.

FIND TREASURE!
Move ahead _____ Space(s).
(Pick a number less than 4 here!)

in Venice

Move ahead **3** spaces.

Escape the **FANG**-tastic monster! Do a happy dance to
_____ .
(Write the title of a favorite song here.)

Move ahead **1** space.

Swap places with another player.

Gondola springs a leak! Go back **2** spaces.

Stop to watch gondola demolition derby! Lose your next turn.

Go back _____ space(s). (Pick a number less than **3** here.)

Send another player back **2** spaces.

Take a break to feed the monster. Lose your next turn.

Finish

77

Turn the page when you're done playing!

You put on a fancy jacket and bow tie and pick up your violin again. You decide that with the tea and the board game, your dad will be fine with the twins looking after him. But as you say goodbye, you're not so sure that YOU are going to be fine. You're hit by the strange feeling that something bad might be about to happen.

I'm sorry to say that feeling is absolutely correct—this IS the evening of April 14 on the <u>Titanic</u>, after all.

You shake off the feeling and head out the door. As long as you keep a low profile, you should be able to pull this off. That's just what you're thinking as you close the cabin door and—

"Pardon me!" a commanding voice calls from behind you. "You with the violin!"

Uh-oh.

You turn. It's a woman with a stuffed fox wrapped around her neck. The poor animal's eyes are open and seem to be watching you.

Your stomach clenches. Your first test is already here! First-class passengers have copies of the White Star Line music book and can request any of its 352 songs on the spot! Every musician is expected to have memorized ALL of the songs.

The woman holds out the book and points to a page. "I want you to play this song. NOW."

You have no choice! Time to play!

Go to the next page.

First, fill in these words:

Funny
adjective

Bob
name

ate
past-tense verb

Cheese
food

Ran
past-tense verb

Scary
adjective

New York
noun

Driving
verb ending in -ing

When you're done, →
fold over this flap.

79

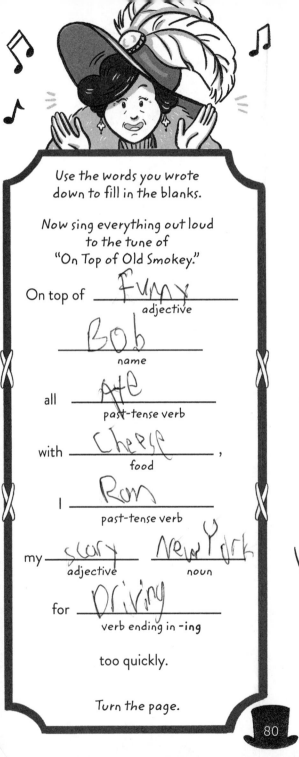

Use the words you wrote
down to fill in the blanks.

Now sing everything out loud
to the tune of
"On Top of Old Smokey."

On top of _Funny_
adjective

Bob
name

all _Ate_
past-tense verb

with _Cheese_ ,
food

I _Ran_
past-tense verb

my _scary_ _New York_
adjective   noun

for _Driving_
verb ending in -ing

too quickly.

Turn the page.

You play so well the woman claps and sings along. "Oh, that's lovely, just like my mother used to sing!" she says, and then she strides off.

Relieved, you make your way to the second-class dining room. It serves pretty much the same food as first class, just not as many courses and without as much hoopla. Still, the passengers are wearing tuxedos and fancy gowns.

The other four musicians in the orchestra raise an eyebrow or two when you explain that your dad's sick. But they're friends with your dad and are happy to help cover for him. Besides, you can really play! And for the next few hours, time just FLIES BY!

Go to the next page.

After dinner, you want to go check on your dad. But the steward in charge tells you and the band to keep playing in a fancy area called the Palm Court.

You're playing "Oh, You Beautiful Doll" at 11:39 p.m. for a small group of sleepy passengers when you hear three notes on a bell.

Ding! . . . Ding! . . . Ding!

But there's not a bell in the orchestra. Maybe it came from someplace on the ship?

Somewhere high in the air, perhaps? Somewhere like the crow's nest?

A minute later, at 11:40, you feel a change in the ship, and it's so dramatic that you play the first wrong notes of the night.

The music of the humming ship you've felt up through your feet for days is GONE. The engines of the *Titanic* have been turned off!

What's happening? you think in a panic as your bow slips off the violin. It knocks into a passing bellhop, who stumbles and dumps a bowl onto a lounging passenger.

Draw a bowl of cold and slimy noodles on a passenger's head.

Now turn the page.

The angry man and several passengers shout and leap to their feet, but the other musicians just keep playing. They've learned over the years to continue no matter what. That's when the steward rushes into the room. You think he's here to throw you into the brig, and then he says the words you'll never forget:

"The *Titanic* has struck an iceberg. We're taking on water."

This must be the exception to the musicians' rule, because they stop playing. In fact, everything stops. For a moment, no one moves and no one breathes. It's so quiet you could hear ANYTHING drop—even if it fell from the top of a skyscraper.

Draw the lightest thing you can think of to drop from this building.

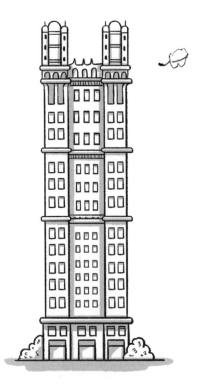

Go to the next page.

A woman gasps. The spell is broken, and chaos erupts in the room. Several people race out the door to find their families or discover what's going on.

A panicked man jostles your violin out of your hand and crushes it under his foot. You're worried someone will get hurt in this mini stampede. You know that music has the power to calm people. But you don't have an instrument!

Wait. Maybe you do. You once saw someone perform using water glasses. You could do the same thing!

A few notes of the song "She'll Be Coming 'Round the Mountain" flutter in your head. They look like this:

DEGGGGED

Quick, run the tip of your pen or pencil around the rims of the glasses in the order of the notes.

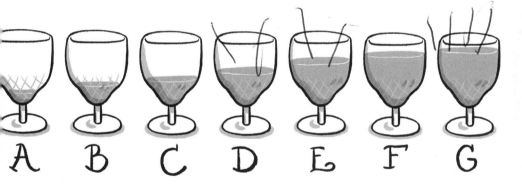

A   B   C   D   E   F   G

TIMER #1

How many of the glasses do you use exactly twice? Write the number here. ———→

Take this number with you to the next page. You're going to need it as you decide when to leave the dining room.

Turn the page.

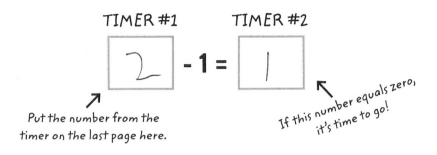

TIMER #1   TIMER #2

2 −1 = 1

↗
Put the number from the
timer on the last page here.

↖
If this number equals zero,
it's time to go!

The remaining passengers and crew seem too stunned to move. One woman announces that an iceberg isn't the problem. She says a four-headed sea monster has attacked the ship! You want to show her how ridiculous that is. . . .

But do you leave now instead? Go to page 86.

If you take the time to draw the monster attacking the ship, do it here. Then go to page 97.

You and three survivors balance on top of the upside-down lifeboat as you wave the blanket high in the air.

You hear shouting coming from a nearby lifeboat! Soon those passengers are making room for you, and you squeeze on board their craft.

Don't forget to draw yourself on the lifeboat!

Turn to page 172.

You run out of the Palm Court, pushing past the other passengers. You NEED to find your dad and the twins and get off this ship! Now!

As you give one last hard shove, the crowd in front of you clears, and you find yourself rushing uncontrollably toward the railing. You hit it and flip forward. You tumble head over heels toward the water below.

Your wish has come true: You're off the ship!

END

Head back to the Palm Court on page 84 and **go-pher** a different choice!

Being careful not to push or shove anyone, you hurry out of the Palm Court. On the deck, crew members are uncovering the lifeboats. Things are much, much worse than you thought. The *Titanic* must be sinking. You need to escape this ship!

Not without my dad and the twins, you think.

Desperate to find them, you rush to your cabin—but it's empty! No one is there.

And your dad's violin is gone. Has he gone below to help your friends find their mom? Maybe, but why would he take his violin? And why didn't he leave you a note? How long do you have before the *Titanic* sinks?

So many questions run through your head. . . . You feel like there's a group of crazed question marks eating up all your thoughts!

Draw question marks gobbling up everything here.

Turn the page.

To get answers, you run down the stairwell to third class—or try to.

The accordion gates separating third class from the higher decks are locked. There's an officer standing guard, and he's telling hundreds of passengers to remain below—that means no one in third class is being allowed up to the lifeboats!

Normally, the roar of the engines down here would be unbelievably loud and make it hard to think. But not after the collision with the iceberg. The only sounds are the confused questions of scores of passengers.

Go to the next page.

"What is happening?" "Are we sinking?" "Why won't you let us out?"

And many other questions in languages you don't understand.

But the officer in charge isn't giving any answers. Instead, he orders everyone to stay away from the barrier... and wait.

There is NO time to wait. You need to find your dad and your friends NOW!

You back away from the gate. After a minute's search, you spot a hatch in the floor that's over third class.

First draw a handle
on this hatch.

Now tear along the dotted lines so
you can swing the hatch open.

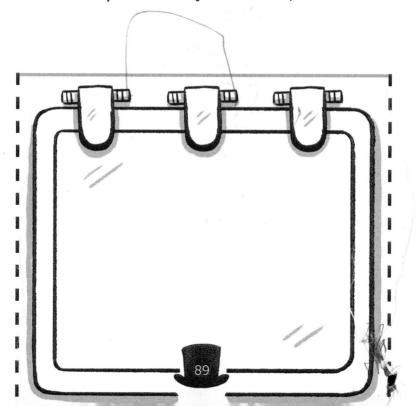

You've waited too long! Now you're in a REAL panic!

Draw yourself running and turn to page 87.

Draw yourself on this flap looking
down through the hatch!
Then turn to page 92.

You slip through the open hatch into third class. You drop to the floor and take a look around. You've landed in the bathing area. Luckily, the room is empty!

There are only two bathtubs—one for men, one for women—for the 709 third-class passengers.

Out in the hall, a sign points in two directions.

← DINING ROOM THIS WAY

THIS WAY TO COMPARTMENTS →

Suddenly, you know just where to look!

Where would the twins most likely be?
Hmm, gee, I wonder. . . . Turn the page.

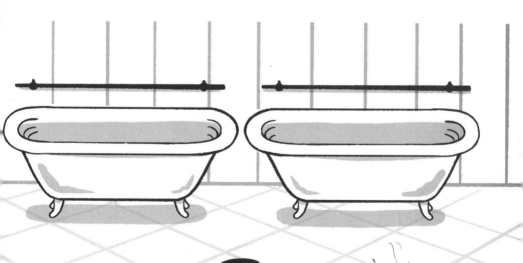

You pop your head into the galley to look around. Then, like the sweetest music ever, you hear Nicola call your name. There are the twins! They're standing over a mixing bowl with a woman you assume is their mother.

"Nicola! Dante!" you shout, and run to them.

They're grinning and are so happy to see you! With the few English words they know, the twins introduce you to their mom and explain that they are trying to calm their nerves by making cookies.

What is wrong with them? Why are they baking when the ship is sinking?

I bet I know. . . . No one has told the third-class passengers how much danger the ship is in.

"Have you seen my dad?" you ask, trying not to panic them.

"No," they say. And then, using a few words in English, plus gestures, the twins explain that your dad started to feel better after you left. Carrying his violin, he walked the twins down to third class and said he was going to take over for you. This was all before the officers locked the gates.

Go to the next page.

"Oh," Nicola says. "He left note."

"My dad left me a note?" you ask. "Where is it?"

The twins apologize that it got mushy when the cookie batter splashed on it. Luckily, they read the note as your dad wrote it. They don't know all the words in English. But they can draw you a rebus of the note.

Quick! What does the message from your dad say?

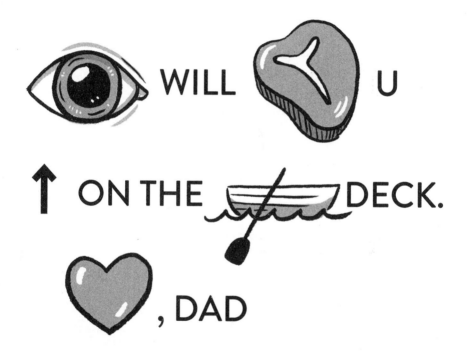

WILL   U

↑ ON THE 🚣 DECK.

♥ , DAD

I will meet you on the boat deck. Love, Dad.

Write the message here.

Need help? Go to page 183.

Turn the page.

"You have to come with me up to meet my dad on the boat deck," you say to the twins and their mom.

Dante shakes his head. "But . . . officer said wait. That all fine."

"No. You can't," you tell him. "It's not safe down here. We need to go right now!"

The twins and their mom—along with a few other people who overheard your conversation—follow you out of the galley back to the hatch you opened. But the hatch has been closed and locked from the other side!

Don't panic. Find a way to convince the officer to open the gate.

As you hurry down the corridor, more and more people join you, until there are a couple hundred passengers following you. When you get to the gate, though, the officer is gone. He must've gone up to the lifeboats!

Find a way out. It's not just you now—there are a lot of people depending on your next move!

The gate is made of interlocking steel strips. It's too tough to break. But a sharp tool could poke through the lock.

If only you had a pointy object in your hand . . .
(Oh wait, you do!)

Poke through the lock to destroy it!

95

Turn the page.

Now you have to open the gate to let everyone through!

Fold the page so that A and B touch each other at the top and bottom to see what page to turn to next.

GO BACK!

THIS WAY TO

BERTHS

154 — 169

PAGE 10 IN YOUR HANDBOOK:

"INSTRUCTIONS FROM CREW MUST BE OBEYED"

Need help? Go to page 18

The number from Timer #2 goes here. ↘

TIMER #2   TIMER #3

\ - 1 = 0

A new crew member has arrived. He's wearing a life jacket, but he's telling everyone to stay calm. "There's nothing wrong!" he says. "The *Titanic* can't possibly sink."

Do you stay to listen to more? Turn to page 90.
Do you leave now? Flip to page 87.

The ship suddenly tilts sideways and slants down as the wounded bow continues to take on thousands of gallons of seawater through giant gashes left by the iceberg. Some passengers seem as if they're in shock or quietly resigned to going down with the ship. Others are pushing—desperate to get on one of the few remaining lifeboats. Many of the boats have already been lowered into the water—and it's clear now that hundreds and hundreds will be left stranded on the sinking ship.

When it comes to getting a spot on a lifeboat, it's women and children first! You lead the twins and their mother to one of the boats. You wonder if this is the very one where you first met them. Their mom climbs aboard and holds out her hand to the twins . . . and you.

Go to the next page.

"Come!" the mother says, clearly wanting to say more but not knowing the English words.

"No, I can't," you say. "I need to find my dad."

"Maybe he is gone," Dante says. "On lifeboat."

You don't think so. You might be young enough to get on a lifeboat, but how will you get your dad off the ship?

"I have to stay," you say.

Dante and Nicola each give you a long hug goodbye. *"In bocca al lupo,"* Nicola whispers in your ear. And then in English, "Good luck."

You have time for one last picture for the twins.
Draw something fun you did together so they'll
always have a good memory of you.

Then turn the page.

With one last wave, the twins are lowered in the full lifeboat down to the water. You need to find your dad!

Not really thinking, you rush inside to the Grand Staircase. You fly down one flight of stairs and look around the lobby. You don't see him anywhere. The ship tilts forward even more. China slides off tables, and chairs tip over.

This was not a good move. You need to head back up.

But when you get to the last landing, where the staircase splits in two, which way will you go?

Go to the right? Turn to page 144.
Do you choose left? Flip to page 45.

WARNING!
This decision can make the difference between your escape's success and failure! Flip to the Escapologist Files to be sure you're armed with the knowledge you need.

PAGE
176

The watertight door lowers shut before you can get out of the room. You're stuck inside . . . and the water is rising!

END

Go-pher a happier ending!
Turn back to page 44
and try again.

It's your boss. And he looks furious. Before you can answer, he says, "Forget it. I don't have time to listen anyway. I need you to run this message to Captain Smith. Now. And wait to see if he has a response he'd like to send!"

He hands you a marconigram—that's a telegraphed message—before rushing off in a huff.

Your heart skips a beat. You've never actually met Captain Smith! He's the highest-paid captain in the world, and he's commanded every maiden voyage of the White Star Line for the past eight years. Some of the globe's wealthiest travelers will only cross the ocean if he's at the wheel.

You're hurrying up to the bridge to deliver the message, when—

You see Captain Smith out strolling along the boat deck with Mr. Ismay, the owner of the White Star Line and pretty much the *Titanic* itself.

There he is!
There's Captain Smith!

Go to the next page.

102

"Sir!" you say, hoping your voice sounds strong. "A message for you!"

Captain Smith takes the marconigram. As he reads it, you wait to see if he will want to send a response. You stare ahead, standing as straight and as proud as you can—like the good naval officer you hope to be someday.

Captain Smith reads the message for a second time and then shows it to Mr. Ismay. Meanwhile . . . you feel a sneeze coming on. Oh no! This is not the time for that! You need to stay still and dignified. But you can tell the sneeze is building and building.

I find that imagining the worst
can sometimes help it NOT to happen.

Try imagining the worst sneeze you can. What would it look like?
Draw it here and then turn the page.

Luckily, MY plan works! The sneeze passes.

Arguing over something in the marconigram, the two men step away toward the railing. The wind is blowing hard off the Atlantic and garbles some of what they're saying.

Unscramble the windblown letters so the words make sense.

Need help?
Go to page 183.

Captain Smith:

This marconigram is a **N G I R N A W** _____ .

We're entering a region with **C E I B R G S E** _____ .

We need to **W L S O** _____ down!

Mr. Ismay:

I don't want to **R H E A** _____ it.

Maintain ship's **D P E E S** _____ !

Frustrated, Captain Smith pushes the marconigram into Mr. Ismay's hands. He barely glances at it and puts it in his pocket. They walk away without another word. For a moment, you're too stunned to move. . . . The *Titanic* could be in danger! You'd better warn the Mortimers!

Go to the next page.

After a quick search, you find Mr. and Mrs. Mortimer already in the dining room at a cozy table for two. They must have left the baby in their suite with the nanny.

Eager to warn them about the icebergs, you hurry toward their table. But Mrs. Mortimer waves you away. She does NOT want to be bothered during dinner. Unsure what to do, you stand in the corner and wait for dinner to be over... and wait... and wait.

Like other passengers in first class, the Mortimers are savoring a ten-course meal, including oysters, salmon, chicken, lamb, duck, squab, filet mignon, and sirloin of beef.

R.M.S. "TITANIC"
First-Class Menu

First Course: _____

Second Course: _____

Third Course: _____

What three courses (or favorite foods) would you serve at an elegant meal? Write them here and then turn the page.

You hold back a yawn. It's 11:35 p.m. Most passengers are in bed by now. But the Mortimers insist that they want a nice SLOW dinner.

You're so tired, you've nearly forgotten about the iceberg warning. You just want to get back to your cramped interior bunkroom and go to sleep.

Finally dinner is wrapping up! Normally the men would go to the first-class smoking room, and the women would head off to the first-class lounge to play cards and chat. But tonight the Mortimers decide they'll listen to music in a fancy room called the Palm Court.

Once Mrs. Mortimer is settled in her overstuffed chair and the orchestra has started playing, you think, *Now's my chance!*

You move toward Mrs. Mortimer to tell her about the icebergs.

GONG! GONG! GONG!

What was that? No one else seems to have heard anything, but you'd swear you just heard the bell in the crow's nest toll three times. As a crew member, you know what it means.

Three bells means danger directly ahead.

The *Titanic* shudders under your feet, and then—

A musician knocks into you, and you spill a bowl of cold noodles on one of the passengers.

It's a mess!

106

Go to the next page.

You feel awful about the accident. If you could give the passenger a gift as an apology, what would it be? Draw it here.

Turn to page 150.

There must be people swimming in the water who couldn't get on a lifeboat and jumped off the *Titanic* as it was sinking. You need to help them. They won't survive long in this freezing water.

One of the older passengers reaches to extinguish the lamp on the lifeboat. "It's too bright," he says.

"No! What are you doing?" you say. The lamp is ten inches high and six inches wide. It's supposed to be bright. "Rescuers won't be able to find us without it. And neither will anyone who had to jump off the ship!"

Your last sentence makes the man even more determined to put out the lamp.

So that's it!
He's worried that swimmers who are
desperate for help will swamp the boat.

Your dad orders the passenger to stay away from the lamp. You decide that, no matter what, you're going to keep this lamp shining bright for any who need help.

Draw a stick with a lamp on the end! When you're done drawing, tear along the dotted lines and turn up the flap to see what the light reveals.

You spot a person who's floating on top of a folding chair from the deck of the *Titanic*! With your dad's help, you pull the person onto the lifeboat. A woman takes off her warm coat and wraps it around the freezing newcomer.

Just then, you turn to see another lifeboat drifting toward you. This one has flipped over, and several survivors are balancing on top.

Everyone—even the passenger who wanted to put out the light—squeezes together to make room for them. An hour later, rockets dot the horizon.

"That's the rescue ship!" your dad says.

Turn the page.

Draw the rockets here. They look like fireworks.

Turn to page 172.

Nicola picks up two napkins from a nearby table. She holds them out like mini flags and starts making shapes with her arms.

*I know what she's doing! That's semaphore!
It's a kind of alphabet—you make letters with your arms.*

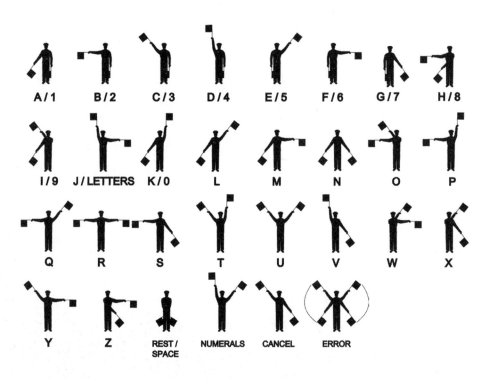

A/1 B/2 C/3 D/4 E/5 F/6 G/7 H/8

I/9 J/LETTERS K/0 L M N O P

Q R S T U V W X

Y Z REST / SPACE NUMERALS CANCEL ERROR

The girl spells out

_____ _____ _____ _____ _____ _____

↑
Write the letters here.

112

Turn to page 70.

I'm sad to say that you've gone the wrong way. You're outside on one of the decks—but you have no idea which one!

"What is this?" a voice demands behind you. Uh-oh. It's Mrs. Mortimer. And she does *not* look happy.

Glancing down at the bundle in your arms, you sputter, "Um, this is your—"

"No, no," she snaps. "I don't mean my precious cargo! You're clearly lost. I can't believe I ever wanted to hire you!"

As she chastises you, you back up. And then back up some more. Before you know it, you've tripped, dropped the "precious cargo," and tumbled over the railing.

You splash into the cold water and resurface just in time to hear someone shout, "Crew member overboard!" An alarm bell starts ringing.

Hopefully, they'll rescue you in time!

END

But just in case . . . why not let Amicus save the day?

If you were looking for suite 260, turn back to page 127.

Were you searching for the dog kennel on E deck? Return to page 131.

CREW MEMBER PATH

Seriously? You want to be a *crew member*? You know this is the RMS *Titanic* and your odds of survival are VERY low, right?

Okay, okay. Before I let you make that choice, I need you to prove something.

Draw a picture of you lifting the heaviest
thing you can imagine . . . with one finger.
When you're done, go to the next page.

Well, I guess that will do. After all, life on the *Titanic* is one big party, right?

That's true for the passengers around you on the gangway. Covered in furs and jewels, they're boarding the world's largest ship—excited about the luxuries that await them on their voyage. But those treats are NOT for you, crew member!

You're one of the *Titanic*'s three teenage bellhops. As part of your job, you will carry passengers' *heavy* bags—and run errands for them during the voyage.

Time to dress the part. Draw yourself in a bellhop uniform. Don't forget the hat! Now turn the page.

Hmm, decent effort, I suppose. But not exactly.

This is the real uniform. It makes you look older . . . which is a good thing. You had to "exaggerate" your age to get a job on the ship. (The two other bellhops are 14 and 16 years old.)

Draw your face here!

But a little lie is worth it. You need money for your sister's eye operation. Sure, you're only being paid about ten dollars for the whole trip. BUT you also get meals, a place to sleep . . . AND the chance to earn tips! This extra money from passengers can make all the difference in helping your sister.

Look! There she is now with your mother in the crowd on the dock! Your sister's cataracts have gotten so thick, your mother has to point you out to her.

"Come home safe!" your mom says. Of course, you can't hear her voice, but you can read her lips—and you can read her thoughts. She's worried about you. Your dad was a steward on a passenger ship when he got badly hurt during a hurricane. You've promised your mom you won't let the same thing happen to you.

You trace a heart in the air for your mom and sister—and try not to get too emotional.

Go to the next page.

What picture of your family means a lot to you?
Draw it here and then turn the page.

With one last look at your family, you get to work! The first-class passengers are handing over their gigantic tickets to your boss before entering the ship—the tickets are bigger than a regular sheet of loose-leaf paper. (Passengers don't need an ID; just saying the name on the ticket is enough.) Each ticket has a detachable strip along one side. The passenger's name is written on the strip and on the main part of the ticket.

𝕷aunch

OF

White Star Royal Mail Triple-Screw Steamer

"TITANIC"

No...193....

Follow the leash to the name of the correct dog!

Lightning

Flealight

If you got to a dog with the name Flealight, turn to page 25.
Followed the leash to a dog called Lightning? Turn to page 123.

Mr. Mortimer nods in approval after you give the tour. But then he frowns. "This is all well and good, but where are my favorite flowers?"

He points angrily to the empty vase on the sitting room table. You look at the book in his hand, and then you think fast!

Draw Mr. Mortimer's favorite flowers in the vase.

Go to page 131.

122

"Lightning, come here!" you call.

The sound of the little dog's name calms him instantly. He bounds over to you and leaps into the air to lick your face. Laughing, you tumble to the luxurious carpet and wrestle with the playful pup. He has the most adorable streak of white on his snout.

A shadow falls over you. A woman with enough jewelry to sink a ship is pointing a bejeweled finger at you. "I want this one!" she tells your boss, who is standing behind her. "This one will be our bellhop for the entire voyage!"

Your boss agrees instantly, but you hesitate before saying yes. You're not so sure. . . . Better flip to the back to discover more.

PAGE
181

"Well, what do you say?" the woman demands shrilly.

If you say, "No thanks!" go to page 25.
If you say, "At your service, ma'am!" turn the page.

"Oh, I'm so glad you and Lightning get along!" the woman says, and flips a coin your way.

Keep track of your tips by drawing this coin on the Tip-O-Meter. (It's on the → back of the strip you detached from the ticket.) Every cent counts!

Cha-ching! These small tips can add up over the voyage and will help to make up for your low pay.

"I'm Mrs. Mortimer," the woman says. "I'm traveling with my husband and my baby daughter, Tiffany. We only have a nanny, a valet, a maid, and a butler. So as you can see, we're desperate! We have NO ONE to carry our bags!"

Climbing to your feet and brushing yourself off, you chuckle. You can't help it. Mrs. Mortimer's staff is bigger than her family! The woman smiles a little and gives you a wink that says, *I know, I know, I'm completely ridiculous!*

She might have a sense of humor, and you like that!

"Tell me about yourself," she demands. "Why do you have this job?"

You quickly tell her about your sister needing an operation. She nods and then suddenly snaps back into snooty-passenger mode.

"Gather all of our things and bring them to our cabin, if you please!" she demands.

Go to the next page.

Time to get to work! Grab a watch or a timer.
Now find the Mortimers' luggage in this pile in
under 20 seconds. Find 10 pieces of luggage
that have the initial **M** stamped on them!

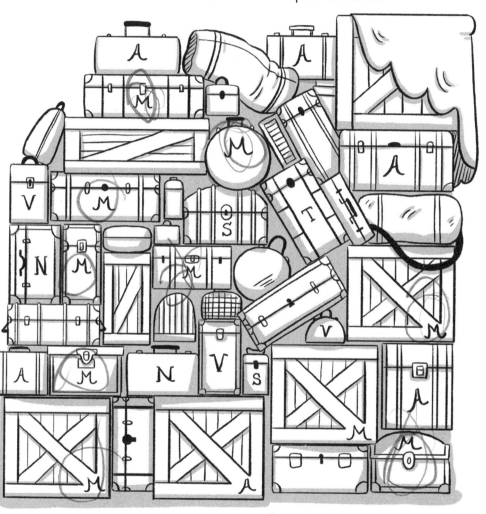

Did you find all the luggage in under 20 seconds? Turn the page.
Longer than 20 seconds? Go to page 170.

You manage to fit most of the Mortimers' luggage onto this covered cart that will be lifted by a motorized crane up to the ship.

How will you squeeze the rest of their things on the cart? If you do it correctly, you'll get the number of the Mortimers' suite. That's where you need to take the luggage. If you mess up, you'll waste valuable time and probably won't get a tip!

Redraw the luggage below in the correct spots on the cart on the next page. Read the number you see from left to right. Use that as a clue to the suite number.

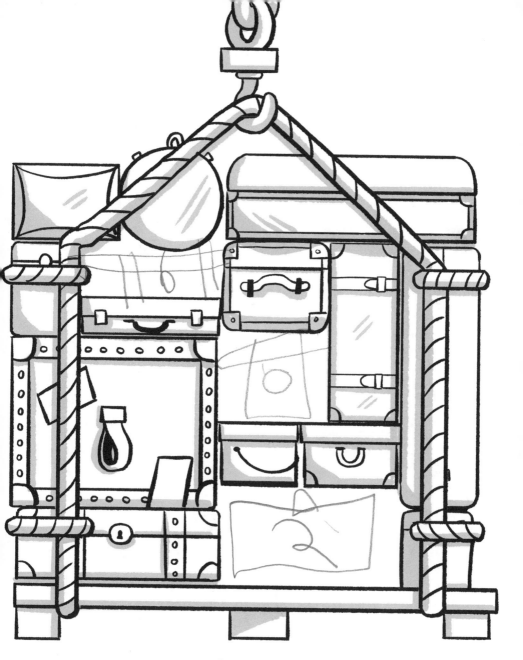

Is it suite 602? Go to the next page.
Or suite 260? Turn to page 113.

There are four elevators on board the *Titanic*—three of them for use by those in first class. You whisk down one of the three first-class elevators from the top deck and arrive on B deck with the luggage. The Mortimer family is standing outside suite 602.

"There you are!" Mrs. Mortimer cries when she sees you pushing the cart down the hallway. "We've been waiting here for two whole seconds!"

Again, you're not sure if Mrs. Mortimer is joking, but just in case, you apologize for being so *horribly* late and open the door for the family. She nods but doesn't give you a tip.

"Let me give you a tour," you say. And you show the family around their enormous suite, which includes two bedrooms, a sitting room, two wardrobe rooms, and a private bath. It has as much space as a small ranch house today—plus they have their own 50-foot-long promenade on the deck that no one else can use.

Time to give the tour! Keep track of where you go by putting your pen (or pencil) to paper. Begin at **START HERE**. Now, without lifting up your pen, follow these directions:

- Go up to the middle of box 4.

- Right to the middle of box 6.

- Follow the line back to box 4.

- Go up to the middle of box 1.

- Right to the middle of box 3.

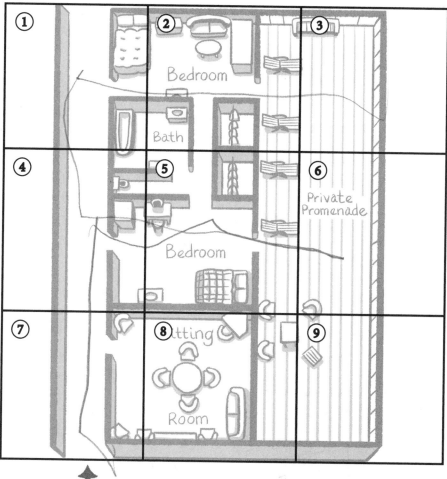

① ② **Bedroom** ③

Bath

④ ⑤ ⑥ **Private Promenade**

Bedroom

⑦ ⑧ ⌐tting ⑨

Room

Start here

What letter did your path through the suite make? Write it here on the Letter Luggage:

When you're done, turn to page 122!

Need help? Go to page 183.

129

"Wrong move!" the master-at-arms says, taking your arm and leading you away.

Welcome to the brig! That's what you call a jail cell on a ship.

Well, it's not really a brig. The *Titanic* doesn't have a jail. So the master-at-arms turned an empty office on a lower deck with no windows into a cell. The only time you see anyone is when a crew member brings you a few slices of bread and some cold soup.

In fact, you're eating when the *Titanic* collides with the iceberg on April 14 at 11:40 p.m. A huge gash is torn in the hull. Icy seawater floods into the ship and into the brig through the crack under the locked door. Water fills the room. Your escape attempt is over!

END

Swallow that last bite of your bread . . . and try again!
Draw Amicus the gopher! If you end up here
more than once, add some color, or shoes, or a hat,
or pants—or whatever!—to Amicus each time.

Did you run left from the master-at-arms? Go right on page 24.

Did you enter the suite? Return to page 21 and change your mind!

Turned down the chief's job? Go back to page 33 and reconsider.

"The flowers are perfect!" Mr. Mortimer says, and flips a coin your way. You catch it and tuck it into your pocket.

Track it on your Tip-O-Meter! ←

PAGE 177

"Yes, they are lovely," Mrs. Mortimer says to you. "But we have more important matters to discuss! A dog show is scheduled on April fifteenth! I intend for Lightning to win Best in Show, and he needs his rest. Take him for a walk and then to the kennel immediately."

At the sound of *kennel*, Lightning lowers his head and nuzzles sadly against your leg.

Everyone else in the family has a room in the suite. The nanny, butler, maid, and valet will all stay in interior cabins nearby.

Why not Lightning? Still, you follow Mrs. Mortimer's instructions. You just hope you can remember where to take him. Which deck is the kennel on?

(Hint: Use the letter from your Letter Luggage on page 129!)

If you choose F deck, go to page 30.
Go to page 113 if you pick E deck.

You climb up your ladder. In seconds, you're at the top—and at a DEAD END. You're standing on the ship's narrow crow's nest, 90 feet above the water.

Luckily, the two lookouts have their backs to you as they scan the horizon. They can see about 12 miles in good weather. If they spot a danger ahead, they'll ring the 15-inch brass warning bell three times and call the captain on the phone that connects from the crow's nest to the ship's bridge.

This is waaaay before ships used radar . . .
so the only collision-avoidance systems on
this ship are human eyes and brains!

PAGE 178

You know the master-at-arms can't be far behind. You hunt for anything to block your face—maybe a pair of binoculars would do the trick? Strangely, there aren't any up here!

Instead you grab an old newspaper that one of the lookouts must have dropped. The front page is about an exotic man-eating plant. You hold the paper over your face as if you're just another lookout reading.

Draw the man-eating plant described in the newspaper! Then go to the next page.

PLANT WITH THREE MOUTHS GROWS AT BASE OF EIFFEL TOWER!

One of the lookouts turns your way and demands, "What're you doing up here?" He sounds furious.

*Let's face it . . . this newspaper disguise
AND the food one maybe weren't the best!*

The lookout is reaching for the phone to call the bridge just as the master-at-arms pushes his way up into the cramped space.

"Don't bother Captain Smith with this, Mr. Fleet and Mr. Lee," the master-at-arms says. "I'll handle it from here." The lookouts hold up their hands, happy to be rid of the problem.

The master-at-arms pulls you back down to the boat deck.

Turn to page 32.

As you're leaving the kennel, one of the other bellhops stops you. "Hey! Mrs. Mortimer is looking for you. She says no one else will do!"

You hustle back to the upper decks. But Mrs. Mortimer isn't in her suite. Where is she?

In the saltwater swimming pool? It's 30 feet long and 14 feet wide, and only the second heated swimming pool on the high seas. The gym? It's equipped with the latest exercise machines, including an electric horse and an electric camel. The squash court? It's the only one of its kind on any ship; for about 50 cents, passengers can rent the court for half an hour. The Turkish bath? Take a break in the steam room, hot room, shampooing rooms, or cooling room. The barbershop? Passengers can get a shave, a shampoo, or a haircut for 25 cents each at one of two swivel chairs. Or the photography darkroom? There you'll find all the equipment that amateurs need to develop the photos they take on the voyage.

See the six numbered boxes on page 135? Redraw each one in the corresponding box in this grid. I've done the first one for you. When you're finished, you'll have a big clue to Mrs. Mortimer's location!

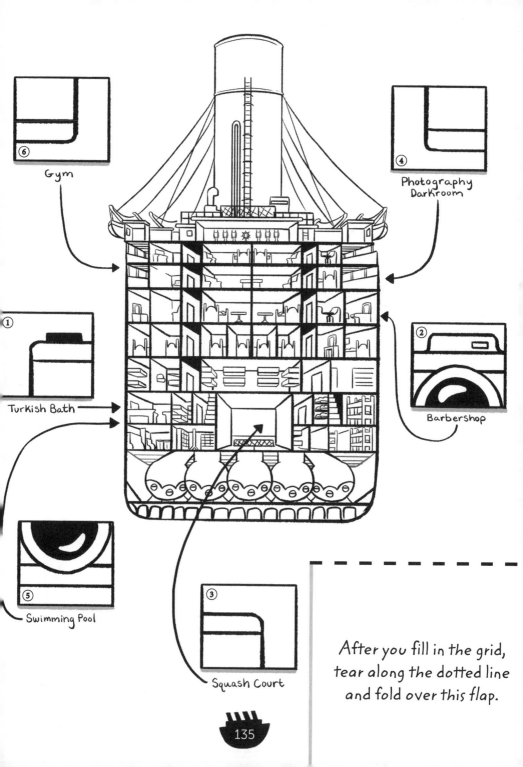

Gym

Photography Darkroom

① Turkish Bath

② Barbershop

⑤ Swimming Pool

③ Squash Court

After you fill in the grid, tear along the dotted line and fold over this flap.

135

"Oh, FINALLY!" Mrs. Mortimer cries when she sees you. "I NEED you to go to the sea post office for me. I want you to mail a photograph that I'm developing. Send it to my mother-in-law in Boston. It's a darling photo of our nanny holding a balloon while riding the electric camel in the gym! Finish developing the photo and then put it in this envelope."

You don't bother to say that the mail won't be able to leave the ship until you reach New York City. You have the feeling she knows that. She just loves creating chaos!

Ah! The camera clue was a giveaway! Turn the page.

Draw the photograph that Mrs. Mortimer described here.
Don't forget the nanny, the balloon,
and the gym's electric camel!

Done with the photo? Aces!
Add the coin she hands you to your Tip-O-Meter
and turn the page.

You head to the sea post office. It stretches out over parts of F and G decks. When you arrive, two men are throwing sacks of mail behind a long counter and three others are carefully sorting through the bags. These clerks of the sea post service—two British and three American—are among the best postal clerks on the planet.

They'll sort, cancel, and redistribute around 60,000 letters a day during the voyage. And they'll have the mail ready to be delivered or forwarded on to the other destinations once the *Titanic* reaches New York.

PAGE **178**

You whistle in wonder at all the mail. One of the clerks looks up from his work and smiles. "These three thousand four hundred and twenty-three sacks contain over seven million pieces of mail. We've been working for the past hour checking all the mailbags and storing away the ones that don't need to be opened on the trip."

"I didn't know mail was such a big part of this voyage," you say.

The American clerk's smile grows bigger. "This is the RMS *Titanic*. RMS stands for *Royal* Mail *Ship*."

Oh! Now I remember. The ship is like a floating post office!

MAIL

MAIL

138

Go to the next page.

You decide to send your own postcard
to your mom and sister while you're here.

Draw your postcard. Maybe make it a picture
of one of your adventures on the ship so far.

Turn to page 41.

April 14, 1912

11:38 p.m.: The lookouts Fleet and Lee see "a black object" that's "high above the water." They ring the warning bell three times and call the bridge.

11:39 p.m.: Captain Smith is in his quarters. At the helm, First Officer William Murdoch gives the order to go around the iceberg: "Hard a-starboard." He then tells the engine room, "Stop. Full speed astern." Basically, ↓ he is trying to put the ship in reverse.

That means to the right.

The 100-ton rudder begins to turn the ship, and the engines start to respond. But it's too late. It will take the *Titanic* about a half mile to stop moving ahead.

11:40 p.m.: That's too long. The iceberg slices open the *Titanic*'s hull.

Turn to page 42.

You try the door handle.
The solid oak door is locked tight!

Think. Think. How will you get inside?

Maybe you don't need to get inside! You left the envelope close
to the door. AND there is a pretty large crack under the door.
You just need something to stick under the door and drag the
envelope along the floor to you.

You can use your pen or pencil!

Tear along the two dotted lines at the bottom of the page.
Keeping this flap closed, stick your pen or pencil under
the crack and mark an X on the next page.

When you're done, turn the page to see
what you've hooked with the X!

Did you get the right envelope?
Keep trying until you do!

After you grab the envelope, turn the page.

Aces! You have the envelope!

You carefully unseal it, take out your postcard, and slide Mrs. Mortimer's photograph in. Just as you're putting the resealed envelope and postcard back under the door, a shadow falls over you.

"What are you doing down here?" an angry voice demands.

Turn to page 102.

Count Vlad
73 Coughing Lane
Impale, Ohio

Mrs. Madeline Mortimer
1 Best Street
Boston, Massachusetts

Alexander H. Emington
24 Shoe Place
Loafer, California

Remember: When you find the right envelope, go to page 142.

You head right, to the starboard side of the boat deck. And you run smack into your dad's orchestra and a few other musicians.

He has tears in his eyes! He's thinking he'll never see you again!

Your dad and the others have been playing for nearly two hours near the exit from the Grand Staircase to calm the passengers.

PAGE 179

Things over on the starboard side *are* less frantic. First Officer Murdoch, the officer in charge, is a little more willing to let men and older boys onto the lifeboats.

"Dad!" you shout. His head jerks up and he swipes away the tears as if he can't believe his eyes.

"You're here!" He drops the violin as he rushes to you. "I thought you left on a lifeboat hours ago! I was happy thinking that you were safe!"

"I couldn't leave without you," you say. The other musicians keep playing as you hug. You feel like your heart might burst with happiness.

Draw your heart playing happily along with the orchestra, and then go to the next page.

144

Your **hug** is interrupted when you're both **shoved** aside. It's J. Bruce Ismay, the man responsible for limiting the **number** of lifeboats on board. He pushes his way past you and your **father**. He **jumps** onto a lifeboat just as it's being lowered to the **water**. You and your dad promise you won't act like that, no matter what!

"Come on," your dad says. "Let's get **you** onto a lifeboat."

There are only three left on this side of the ship, and they're just about to be lowered.

The seven bolded words on this page are hidden in the puzzle. Find them! They might be written up, down, forward, backward, or diagonally. The leftover letters will spell out your next step!

```
T S R U R N Y
N H T E U H O
E O U M T P U
A V B G G A E
R E H T A F W
R D J U M P S
```

After you circle the words in this puzzle, write the leftover letters here and follow the instruction.

____ ____ ____ ____ ____ ____ ____ ____ ____ ____ ____ ____ ____ ____

Need help?
Go to page 183.

The "collapsible" Engelhardt lifeboat you choose is 28 feet long, 8 feet wide, and 3 feet deep and can carry 47 people. It's nearly filled with young children and a few women caring for them.

"Go ahead without me," your dad tells you. "There must be a rescue ship on the way. If not . . . well, tell Mom and your brother I said goodbye, and that I love them."

The bow of the *Titanic* is nearly underwater now. "No!" you say. "With all these kids, we'll need people to row and steer the boat!"

The officer nearby agrees with you. Actually, you're not sure if it's an officer—it looks like it could be a teenage bellhop.

"That's true," the bellhop says. "You can both go. The only possible rescue ship is still miles away. It won't arrive before the *Titanic* sinks."

With a nod of thanks, you and your dad both climb aboard and sit next to each other. From what you can see, you're in one of the last boats. But you know there must be hundreds of people still on the *Titanic*.

The bellhop and other crew members lower your boat using ropes and pulleys.

Draw yourself and your dad in the lifeboat!

Turn the page.

Your boat hits the water with a splash! One of the two bright lamps tumbles off the side, and there's a terrifying moment where you think the whole lifeboat might capsize. Waves slam the lifeboat up against the *Titanic*'s hull, and many of the children on board scream.

You and your dad do your best to calm them down. You each grab an oar, put it into the water, and start rowing your boat away from the *Titanic*.

The rowing is hard! Show that you can keep the oar in the water as you row. Poke the tip of your pen or pencil up through the white circle from the other side of the page. Then move it back and forth.

Leave at least five swipe marks here!

148

Now go to the next page.

Lucky for those on your lifeboat, you and your dad row quickly away from the *Titanic*. Fortunately, you avoid being sucked underwater as the great ship sinks about 15 minutes later—its electric lights finally going out and its hull cracking in two.

It's a horrible sight, and something you will never forget.

149

Turn to page 108.

The passenger wearing the latest noodle fashion is outraged! A few of the other passengers chuckle. Mrs. Mortimer opens her mouth to really let you have it. But she sees the look on your face, and her expression changes from anger to worry. Before she can say anything, your boss rushes into the Palm Court.

"The ship has struck an iceberg!" he shouts.

I might have delivered the news a little differently.

A murmur of concern comes from the passengers and crew. But the musicians keep playing, so it's hard to get too scared.

"Will the ship . . . ?" one woman asks, clearly not wanting to say the word *sink.*

"Of course not," another passenger says.

"I'm not so sure," your boss says.

Forget a gentle murmur. Now the passengers erupt with panic.

Imagine if worry were lava . . . and draw an erupting volcano of worry here!

Go to the next page.

"Stay calm, everyone!" your boss finally says. "Stay calm!"

But it's too late. Mrs. Mortimer is on her feet.

"Come along, darling," she says to her husband. "We need to get the baby and get to a lifeboat—"

"Ma'am!" a loud voice calls. It's the Mortimers' nanny, standing just inside the doorway. Her face is red, and she's holding the Mortimers' baby. Behind her are their butler, maid, and valet.

"Okay, we're all here," Mrs. Mortimer says, and begins herding her family and staff out of the room. "If you're smart, you'll get to the lifeboats," she tells you and the other passengers. "NOW."

"What about Lightning?" you call after the Mortimers. But they're not listening and have already left the Palm Court.

Surely there is time to get the dog out of the kennel on F deck. Time cannot be that precious, can it?

Unfortunately, it is.
You have less than an hour before
you'll be trapped forever on the <u>Titanic.</u>

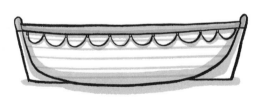

If you decide to get Lightning, turn to page 153.

If you decide to go straight to the lifeboats, turn to page 12.

You reach for the handle of the door. Without hesitating, you throw it open, dash inside . . .

And find yourself on the bridge of the *Titanic*. That's where officers steer the boat.

Say hello to Captain Smith for me!

END

All right, all right! So I lied about which hiding place to choose. I promise, no more tricks. Everything I tell you from now on will be true. Maybe.

You can go back to page 11 and make a different decision. This is a one-time offer! My gopher, Amicus, might help you in the future, but not I!

Lightning, here I come! you think.

You hurry out onto the boat deck and start making your way to the kennel on F deck. You hear barking . . . lots and lots of barking!

A pack of dogs is racing up and down the deck in a panic. Someone must have set the kennel dogs free. You scan their faces, looking for Lightning.

Do you see him?

Fold up the flap.

You rush down the Grand Staircase toward F deck. Scared clumps of passengers wearing life jackets from their rooms are coming the other way. You have to weave through the crowd. People see your uniform and pepper you with questions. "What's happening? Is this a drill?" they demand. "Are we in danger?"

"I'm not sure," you tell them honestly. "Please remain calm and make your way to the boat deck."

There's no public address, or PA, system on the *Titanic* to spread word to passengers and crew about what's happening. The ship's stewards have been going from cabin to cabin telling each passenger. But apparently they haven't been telling them much—only to go to the boat deck with their life jackets.

You should follow your own instructions to stay calm.
Think about a place that makes you feel peaceful. Draw it here.

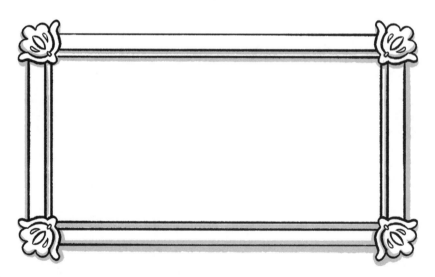

No, there's no sign of
lightning. Turn the page!

Go to the next page.

You fly down the stairs to F deck. The door to the kennel is unlocked. Inside, all the cages are open . . . except one.

At first you don't see anything inside, and then you hear a whimper. Lightning is still in his crate, scared and trembling. Louis must have missed him hiding in the back!

You need to get him out, but the crate is locked. Where did Louis store the key? You watched him put it away when you were here before.

Do you remember where???

You don't have time to choose the wrong spot. Right now water is flooding into the bow of the *Titanic* where it struck the iceberg. Flip over the correct flap to find the key—hurry!

Time is money. . . .
If you pick the wrong spot,
you'll have to deduct a coin
from your Tip-O-Meter!

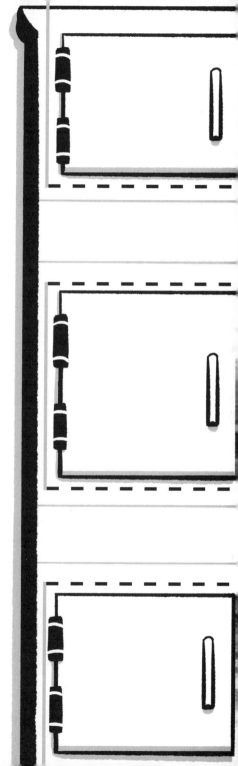

Cross out one
coin from your
Tip-O-Meter.
The key is NOT here!

You've done it!

The cage flies open, and Lightning leaps out into your arms. You give him a quick squeeze as his tongue happily licks your face.

No time for a reunion party. You need to get out of here!

The floor under your feet tilts as the *Titanic* continues to sink—and the hallway is filling with cold seawater.

*I know what would keep
you up out of the water!
Draw yourself walking
on a pair of stilts.*

Success!
You've found the key!
Turn the page.

Cross out one coin
from your
Tip-O-Meter.
The key is not
in this cubby!

Go to the next page.

Holding Lightning tight, you slosh through the freezing water and hurry up to the boat deck. . . .

It's pandemonium. They've started loading the lifeboats—but there's only room for about half of the 2,200 or so people on the *Titanic*. Many are shouting and pushing.

Gunfire explodes as your boss fires his pistol into the air as a warning, trying to get people to listen and calm down. "Women and children first!" he shouts. "The RMS *Carpathia* picked up our distress call fifteen minutes ago—but at that point it was fifty-eight miles southeast of us!"

If he wanted calm, that was not the way to get it.

You spot the Mortimers' bags piled up nearby on the deck. You're surprised that they wasted time getting their luggage!

Reaching into one of the Mortimers' suitcases, you grab a small blanket and swaddle Lightning in it. He looks like a baby—a very *interesting* baby, but a baby nonetheless.

Draw what Lightning looks like in his cozy blanket.

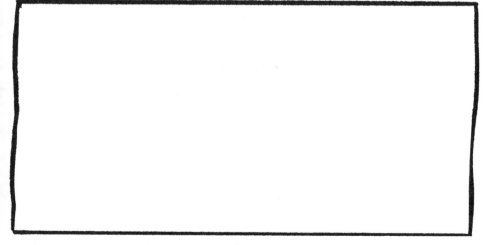

157

Turn to page 74.

The twins want to be chefs in America!

You think that's amazing and nothing to be embarrassed about. Maybe they can get a start in the restaurant owned by your dad's friend. You can't wait to ask your dad what he thinks of the idea!

"Come with me," you tell them, and you lead the twins to your cabin. Your dad has been so busy playing music that you haven't had the chance to introduce him to your friends.

When you open the door of the cabin, you don't find the happy, always-whistling father you know. Instead, you find him collapsed on the bed, green-faced and moaning. He's got a horrible case of seasickness!

When the twins ask what's wrong, you pull out your pad and pen or pencil to explain.

Draw three wild monkeys bouncing on a trampoline in this stomach.

This is what being seasick feels like.

Go to the next page.

Your dad manages to say hello to the twins and then moans, "I'm supposed to play tonight at dinner and then after in the Palm Court. I'm going to get fired when I don't show up."

Without hesitating, Dante picks up your violin and puts it in your hands. When you ask what he's doing, Nicola gives you a gentle push toward the door. They're both nodding at you.

You guess what they're encouraging you to do. "You want me to play in place of my dad? I'll get caught!"

Nicola rolls her eyes at your worry. *"Vivi la vita!"* she says. It sounds something like "Live life!"

"But what about Dad?" you ask. "I can't leave him here alone."

"I'll be fine," your dad says, sitting up in his bed. "You could save my job. I'll need the references if I want to get a good teaching job."

"Special tea," Nicola says in English. After a few quick pictures, you figure out their mother makes a special tea for them when they're not feeling well. They'll get your dad some tea and stay in the cabin with him. They'll even bring up a board game!

To take a quick break and play the twins' board game, turn to page 76.

To stay focused on playing the violin, go to page 78.

At 2:05 a.m. on April 15, you help load passengers into the very last lifeboat and it leaves the *Titanic*.

You've been working so hard for the past hour and a half, you didn't realize how low the *Titanic* is now sitting in the water. The bow is almost completely submerged. Deep in the ship's engine room, boilers are exploding as water floods into them.

There's no more time.
Either you make your escape NOW
or you will go down with the ship.

That's when the *Titanic* begins to slide into the water.
The stern rises up in the air.

Sailors call the back of a ship the stern.

If you run up the sloping deck, go to page 61.
If you stay put, turn to page 162.

A passing bellboy with a trunk over his head turns, accidentally hitting you with it. You're knocked toward the railing. Unfortunately, you strike the railing just right, flip over backward—and fall off the ship.

As you tumble into the cold water below, you think, *I should've tried harder to pick up hints from the Master Escapologist!* You're not allowed back on the boat.

I couldn't have said it better myself. Only those who recognize the great make the great escapes!

Draw your face when you realize you don't get to sail on the <u>Titanic</u>—and have to call Aunt Clemence to come get you!

END

Didn't follow the kid through the crowd? Let's **go-pher** that again. Head back to page 60!

Want to rethink your search for that missing kid? **Go-pher** it again on page 65!

You don't rush aft. Instead, you wait, just a minute longer, until the ship sinks a bit more. When the surface of the water is closer, you dive off the ship.

PAGE 175

You gasp when you hit the freezing water, thinking your heart might actually stop. You swim a few feet away from the ship—

PAGE 177

But then you're pulled back to the hull, sucked against the wire mesh of a giant airshaft that leads down to the engine room. Water is rushing into the shaft as the *Titanic* sinks, and the pressure is sticking you to the wire mesh.

You're going to sink with the ship! You need a blast of air to come OUT of the airshaft and blow you free.

One of the most dangerous plans ever created pops into your head. But it just might work!

Follow the maze of pipes from the exploding boiler in the engine room to the airshaft. The numbers you cross will tell you what page to go to next.

Need help?
Go to page 183.

FINISH

4

8

5

6

Turn to page

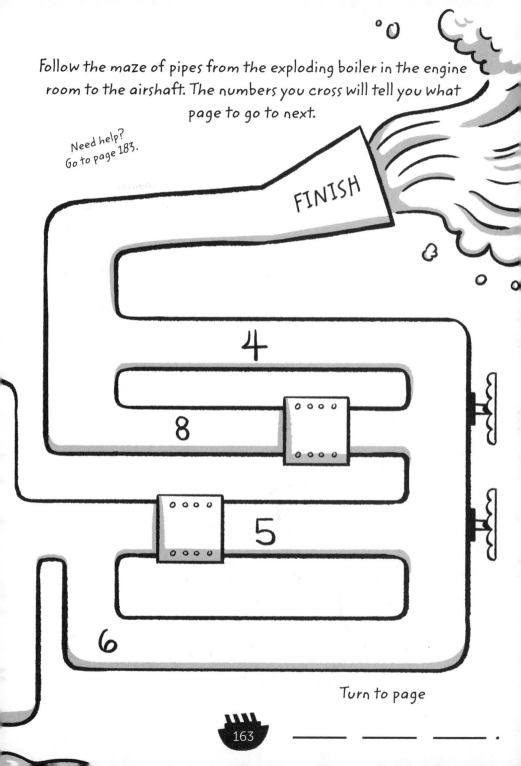

ACES! YOU'VE DONE IT!

Hot air erupts out of the shaft and shoots you back to the surface.

You're pulled under one more time by the suction of the sinking ship. When you come back up again, you're next to an overturned lifeboat.

You hold on to a piece of rope attached to the lifeboat and pull yourself onto the back of the craft. Well done. But I'm afraid you're not safe yet.

One of the ship's four 60-ton smokestacks—each one about 22 feet wide and 6 stories high—cracks off.

You watch it fall toward you as if it's moving in slow motion.

WHAM!

The smokestack slams into the water just a few feet from you!

Turn to page 49.

So much of the ship is underwater that it's flowing over the tall bulkheads. Water is actually coming down on you as you run up the stairs. Scotland Road is now a river. Water rushes through the long corridor, pouring into nearly every section of the ship.

It's so hard to find your way up to the boat deck, where the lifeboats are. Water seems to be flowing from all directions.

Connect the dots to reveal the page to turn to next.
You can trust me this time, I promise!

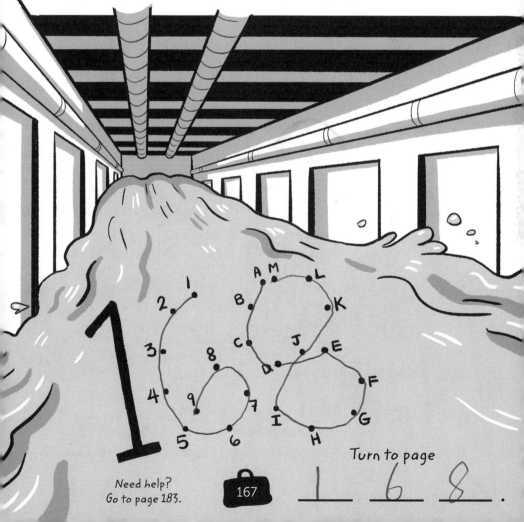

Turn to page 1 6 8 .

Need help?
Go to page 183.

By the time you reach the boat deck, it's two in the morning and the last lifeboat is being lowered down the side of the *Titanic*. You quickly realize that the Italian boy and girl would have figured out what was going on—or you hope they just stayed put in the lifeboat and are now in the water a safe distance away.

Not to worry, I can see them. . . . They're on a lifeboat already!

From up here, it's very clear that the *Titanic* has just minutes left. The ship's bow is sinking deeper and deeper into the water, causing the deck to tilt more and more.

You look over the railing. The last lifeboat is about halfway to the water. You could still get on it . . . if you really wanted to try.

If you jump down onto the lifeboat, turn to page 53.
If you decide to devise your own way to escape, go to page 51.

After you smash the lock and push the accordion gate open, you make your way up to the boat deck, with your friends and a hundred or so passengers streaming behind you.

You come out on the port side . . . and it's mayhem!

Turn to page 98.

"I'm very sorry," you tell Mrs. Mortimer in her cabin. "I made a slight mistake. . . ."

Before you can explain, Mrs. Mortimer holds up her hand to silence you. She then shoos you out the door and slams it shut.

Um, I guess she doesn't like the word *mistake*. You know who else doesn't? Your boss! He's in the hallway, and he's heard everything.

Without waiting for your side of the story, he says, "You've angered one of our most important passengers! It's toilet-cleaning duty for you!"

END

Ugh. That might be worse than actually hitting an iceberg!
Let's try that again.

Want to fix your mistake in the post office? Go back to page 41.

Were you trying to find all of the Mortimers' luggage? Return to page 125.

"I thought you knew about coal," Mr. Bell says, shaking his head at the mistake you just made. "It's too dangerous for you down here in the engine room after all."

"Where else can I go?" you ask.

"Into the brig until the voyage is over," Mr. Bell responds. "It will be the safest spot on the ship for you."

Now he's the one making a mistake. *No spot on the ship will be safe . . .* once the *Titanic* hits the iceberg.

Let Amicus help!

Did you shovel coal from the left? Try again on page 37.

Followed the wrong path? Want to find the real source of the fire? Return to page 39.

The RMS *Carpathia* has steamed full speed through the dangerous ice field for nearly 60 miles—passing six icebergs—to get here as quickly as possible.

The *Carpathia* arrives at 4 a.m., and for the next four hours it rescues the *Titanic* survivors—including YOU.

You can't believe you're one of the lucky ones who are now safely setting sail to New York.

Well done! You have made your escape!

Track your progress when you finish
escaping in each of the three roles.

Draw yourself as the
happy stowaway here.

Draw yourself as the victorious passenger here.

Draw yourself as the successful crew member here.

I have a special message . . . but only for someone who has shown promise as a true escapologist!
Turn back to page 7 to try another path.
When you complete ALL THREE paths, turn to page 174.

Congratulations are in order! You have done well and have escaped one of my most difficult challenges.

My name is Evolo Cherishwise. Yes, yes, I'm sure you have heard of me. I am, after all, the universe's Supreme Escapologist. No one else's skills come close to mine!

Still . . .

Every now and then even a Master Escapologist can use some assistance. And that's where you come in. Continue to prove yourself as a valuable Apprentice Escapologist through my challenges—and I will reveal to you the most ultimate of secrets!

Until then . . . make each escape great!

Evolo Cherishwise,
Master Escapologist

ESCAPOLOGIST FILES

SHIPSHAPE MAGAZINE

April 1912

Here's how to find your way around the *Titanic*— the largest moving object humans have ever made!

PORT (Left side) BRIDGE

← CROW'S NEST

AFT

STERN

BOW

STARBOARD (Right side)

ASK ANVIL!

DEAR ANVIL:

How did the poop deck get its name?

Signed,
Curious in Columbus

DEAR CURIOUS:

The name probably didn't start how you think! The poop deck is usually located in the stern. Some people say that its name comes from the French word for stern—*la poupe* (which comes from *puppis,* the Latin word for boat or stern).

Yours in Answers,
Anvil

DECISIONS MAGAZINE

Is It the Right Way to Live? Or the Left?

One landing of the *Titanic's* Grand Staircase had doors that led out to the ship's deck. One doorway was on the right, and the other was on the left. For some passengers on the night of April 14, 1912, the decision of which way to go would determine whether they escaped the sinking ship.

On the port side, Second Officer Charles Lightoller was in charge of getting people into the limited number of lifeboats. He was very strict about the "women and children first" rule. No men were allowed to board. He even tried to block 13-year-old John Ryerson from getting on a lifeboat with his mother. (At the time, 12-year-olds could leave school and get a job, and Lightoller argued that made John a man.) Lucky for John, Lightoller finally allowed him on the lifeboat.

First Officer William Murdoch was in charge of loading the lifeboats on the starboard side. He also followed the rule about women and children first . . . but he was more flexible. When there weren't any women or children waiting for a lifeboat, he allowed men to board. So those passengers looking for the greatest chances of survival would have wanted to head to the starboard side!

STOWAWAY? SOME SAY, "NO WAY!"

Were there stowaways on the *Titanic*? We might never know the answer for sure, but many people argue there weren't any. They point out that all the survivors from the *Titanic* had their names checked against passenger and crew lists by personnel on rescue boats and by immigration officials in the United States. Others say it's not impossible for someone to have slipped past all the checkpoints . . . or perhaps there were stowaways on board that fateful night who were lost when the ship sank.

------ COME TO THE ------
TITANIC DOG SHOW

Sad to say this dog show for the 12 dogs on board never took place. Many believe it was scheduled for April 15, the day the *Titanic* sank.

NOTE TO MY AMAZING SELF:

Be sure to give credit to Charles Lightoller, who served on the <u>Titanic</u>! Much of the end of the crew member path—from being sucked against the mesh grate to the smokestack nearly falling on him—actually happened to this second officer!

·177·

HELP WANTED

Are you a top sea postal clerk? Then we have a job for you! The White Star Line is looking for the world's best five sea postal clerks to serve on the most luxurious ship—the brand new RMS *Titanic*. If you have what it takes, we'll pay you $1,000 a year! Plus, all of your meals will be free, AND we'll even give you an allowance to spend on housing in destination ports while you wait for the return trip.

THE KEY TO DISASTER

FRED FLEET was one of the two lookouts on the *Titanic* who used just their eyes to scan the horizon for any danger. Fleet later said that if the lookouts had been able to use binoculars, he might have seen the iceberg in the ship's path sooner. That would have given the bridge more time to steer the ship around the iceberg—rather than crashing into it.

Making the evening more tragic, the crow's nest actually did have a pair of binoculars. But they were shut tight in a locker, and the key to the locker wasn't on the ship. Just before the ship left for its fateful voyage, Second Officer David Blair was removed from the crew. When he walked off the *Titanic*, he accidentally took the key with him!

TOILET TIMES MAGAZINE
Hands-Free Flushing!

Exciting news on the *Titanic*! Some of the toilets flush automatically. But only in third class. Why? Many think it's because those passengers might not be used to indoor plumbing—they may be more familiar with chamber pots or outhouses (which have no running water, of course). It's possible those passengers don't know they can flush!

PROFILES OF MUSIC LEGENDS
Meet Wallace Hartley!

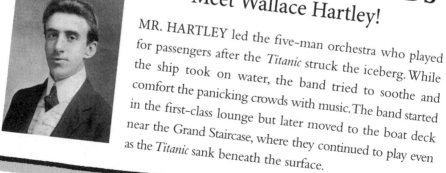

MR. HARTLEY led the five-man orchestra who played for passengers after the *Titanic* struck the iceberg. While the ship took on water, the band tried to soothe and comfort the panicking crowds with music. The band started in the first-class lounge but later moved to the boat deck near the Grand Staircase, where they continued to play even as the *Titanic* sank beneath the surface.

HELP WANTED!

If you want to earn under $30 a month, get really (really!) dirty, and work harder physically than anyone else on the ship—come be a trimmer on the *Titanic*. You'll be on the lowest rung of the social and work ladder, and you'll probably have to work when others get the day off! You'll shovel and evenly distribute heavy piles of coal, keeping the piles trimmed (that's why the job is called trimmer).

Your boss will also order you to degrease machinery, paint spaces under the engine room deck plates—and do whatever other dirty job he can think of! So what do you say? Want the job?

FIRE FACTS: DID YOU KNOW?

ABOUT THREE WEEKS before the *Titanic* left port on its one and only voyage, a large coal fire broke out in its hull—and that fire continued to burn until the ship sank. Some experts believe the *Titanic*'s owners were aware of the fire in the three-story-high bunker next to the ship's boiler rooms—but they chose not to say anything because it would have delayed the ship's departure and cost them a lot of money.

HEROES MAGAZINE

As the ship flooded, many crew members stayed below to work the pumps and keep electricity flowing. Thanks to their bravery, the *Titanic*'s 10,000 lightbulbs stayed lit until just minutes before the ship sank—long enough for nearly all the lifeboats to be lowered into the water.

CAREER COACH

FOR ALL THOSE BELLHOPS out there wondering if they should work for first-class passengers, keep this in mind: First-class passengers expect the best. After all, one of their tickets could cost around $4,350. (That's more than 400 times the amount a bellhop is paid to work on the *Titanic*.) These are some of the richest people on the planet. But that doesn't mean they're always the best tippers.

That's about $100,000 in today's money!

ADDITIONAL EXPLORING

Here are a few of the sources the Master Escapologist
used for research when putting together this adventure.

Books

Donnelly, Judy. *The Titanic: Lost . . . and Found.* New York:
Random House Children's Books, 2010.

Jenner, Caryn. *Survivors: The Night the Titanic Sank.* New York:
DK Publishing, 2001.

Kentley, Eric. *Story of the Titanic.* New York: DK Publishing, 2012.

Stewart, Melissa. *Titanic.* National Geographic Readers.
Washington, D.C.: National Geographic Society, 2012.

Television Documentary

Inside the Titanic
(Dangerous Films/Handel Productions [ITT]/SIA Baltic Film Services/
For Discovery Communications LLC/Discovery Channel Canada/
France Télévisions/BBC Worldwide, 2012)

Websites

nationalgeographic.com/explore/isotry/a-titanic-anniversary
encyclopedia-titanica.org
postalmuseum.si.edu/titanic
smithsonianmag.com/smart-news/definitive-guide-dogs-titanic

ANSWERS

p. 10: The letter for the Letter Luggage is C.

p. 18: ICEBERGS

p. 57: The answer is page 62.

p. 69: The paths are shaped like a 1 and a 2. The page number is 112.

p. 73: The message is: We want to be chefs in America.

p. 93: The note says: I will meet you up on the boat deck. Love, Dad.

p. 96: Go to page 169.

p. 129: The letter for the Letter Luggage is F.

p. 163: Go to page 164.

p. 104

Captain Smith:

This marconigram is a **WARNING**.
We're entering a region with **ICEBERGS**.
We need to **SLOW** down!

Mr. Ismay:

I don't want to **HEAR** it.
Maintain ship's **SPEED**!

p. 134

p. 145

T S R U R N Y
N H T E U H O
E O U M T P U
A V B G G A E
R E H T A F W
R D J U M P S

<u>TURN THE PAGE</u>

p. 167

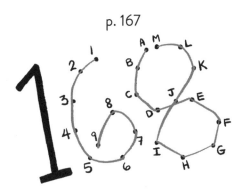

BILL DOYLE

Bill Doyle is the author of <u>Attack of the Shark-Headed Zombie</u> and <u>Behind Enemy Lines,</u> as well as many other books for kids—with over two million copies in print. He has also created lots of games for Sesame Workshop, Warner Bros., and Nerf. He says, "My happiest moment as an author was when the genius Master Escapologist sent me a secret message offering me the job to write his incredible books." (No, he's not just saying that because the Master Escapologist is writing this biography!) Bill lives in New York City and San Francisco, and you can find out more about him at BillDoyleBooks.com.

MASTER ESCAPOLOGIST

Let me put it this way: You don't get named a Master Escapologist unless you are the best . . . and that is exactly what I am. THE BEST! I'm not going to give you any hints here about my true identity. You'll have to make your escape in this book to discover more about me!

SARAH SAX

Sarah Sax is an illustrator and comic artist based in Oakland, California. She cares deeply about how, why, and what people create, and she works to foster the creative spark in makers of all ages. She studied illustration, animation, and storytelling at Hampshire College; has a background in arts education; and volunteers regularly with young creatives at 826 Valencia in San Francisco. You can visit Sarah online at SarahSax.me.

Make your next great escape!

Doodle, decide, and demolish your way
out of an ancient tomb, the underworld,
and an archaeological dig site!